Praise for the Mike Romeo thriller series ...

"Mike Romeo is a terrific hero. He's smart, tough as nails, and fun to hang out with. James Scott Bell is at the top of his game here. There'll be no sleeping till after the story is over."
—**John Gilstrap,** New York Times bestselling author of the Jonathan Grave thriller series

"Mike Romeo is a hard-boiled hero: cage fighter, philosopher, acerbic champion of the underdog. James Scott Bell's series is as sharp as a switchblade." —**Meg Gardiner,** New York Times bestselling author

"Mike Romeo is a killer thriller hero. And James Scott Bell is a master of the genre." —**Tosca Lee,** New York Times best-selling author

... and for the writing of James Scott Bell

"Bell takes his place among the top authors in the crowded suspense genre."
—**Sheldon Siegel**, New York Times bestselling author

"I've always been a fan of James Scott Bell."
—**Terri Blackstoc**k, New York Times bestselling author

"Readers who pride themselves on figuring out the answers before an author reveals them are in for a surprise, too: Bell is very good at keeping secrets." —**Booklist**

"Heart-whamming." —**Publishers Weekly**

"A master of suspense." —**Library Journal**

Also by James Scott Bell

Romeo's Rules
Rome's Way

ROMEO'S HAMMER

A Mike Romeo Thriller

James Scott Bell

Compendium Press

ISBN 10: 0-910355-36-3
ISBN 13: 978-0-910355-36-0

The first and greatest victory is to conquer yourself. To be conquered by yourself is of all things most shameful.
— Plato

But tell me what's to be done, Lord, 'bout the weather in my head.
— Donald Fagen

ROMEO'S HAMMER

SHE WAS BEAUTIFUL and naked and dying.

I was doing my early morning run along the beach that starts at Paradise Cove and turns, like a scimitar, toward the tonier sands of the Malibu Colony. I was living in a mobile unit owned by my rabbi-lawyer friend, Ira Rosen. He said the ocean would do me good. I think he just wanted me as far from the denser population of Los Angeles as possible.

He knows me well.

I was not yet to the rough border between my side of the shoreline and that of the Colony where insane money tries to pretend it's just like real folks. It's where movie stars and producers, internet billionaires and divorced wives of sports team owners, big-shot lawyers and trust-fund babies, all dig their toes on the sandy shore of the blue Pacific. They think their toes should be exclusive. They hate to have people like me—worth about thirty bucks on the open market—jogging past their multi-million dollar homes.

Which is exactly why I do it. Under the laws of man and

nature, the strip where ocean meets shore is not owned by anybody. This has not stopped the privileged few from trying to keep out stragglers with illegal fencing and the occasional bit of human intimidation.

Most people are too cowed by this to resist.

I'm not one of those people.

THE FOG WAS thick and wet with salt air. It was like running in a dream. The whisper of the morning waves was a comfort, and I needed some of that. I was feeling fine until a seagull screeched by, unseen but loud enough to chill some blood.

Then the woman appeared, an apparition, with the body of a Greek statue. Like Venus stepping out of her morning shower.

Only this Venus was staggering like a drunk.

Slowing, I watched her face. I didn't want her screaming or thinking I might try to take advantage of the situation. But she didn't make eye contact with me. She didn't look like she could make eye contact with anything.

I looked past her through the fog to see if there was anyone with her. Some lousy boyfriend, maybe, or a party sister. But we were alone in a gray smoke bubble.

"You all right?" I said, feeling stupid because it was obvious she wasn't.

She said nothing. Her right arm came up a little like she was brushing away a fly. She put one foot in front of the other, unsteady.

"Let me help you," I said.

Her head lolled back. She had long black hair, messy around her face, like kelp. Her mouth started to move. It looked like it had a will of its own. Nothing came out. Her empty eyes met mine for a moment. Then they rolled upward and she stumbled toward the waves.

She fell to her knees in the wet sand.

I took off my T-shirt and put it over her head. She fought me a little but I got her arms through the sleeves and pulled the shirt over her torso.

I put my arms under hers and helped her to her feet. She was almost dead weight.

And then she said something. It sounded like *higog*.

"Higog?" I said. "Someone you know?"

Silence. Her lids were heavy.

"Can you tell me where you came from?" I said. "I can take you back."

Pause. She seemed to be forming a thought. It was as if my words had squeezed into her brain slowly, strained through thick gauze.

Then she cursed and jerked out of my grasp.

She took three steps and fell face down and didn't move again.

I PICKED HER up and put her over my shoulder. This was going to be a great sight if some beach cop or concerned citizen were to see me. An inert girl over a man's shoulder does not exactly advertise all is well. Especially when the woman is mooning the sky.

The fog was my friend.

And I wasn't that far from the Cove. I kept on the wet sand to make the walk easier.

The pier was just coming into view when another runner came toward me out of the fog.

It was a man, maybe my age, good shape. Wearing a Dodgers hat, black tank top and black running shorts.

He looked at me. I looked at him and smiled.

"Too much vodka," I said.

The man nodded, ran past.

I took a look back and saw he was looking over his shoulder at me. He didn't buy it. I wouldn't have either. I wondered how long it would be before he called 911.

I got to the parking lot of the Cove's restaurant and then headed up to the gate kiosk. Our regular guy, Rodney, saw me and came out. He's on the fat side of forty, but always wears a smile.

Except now, looking at the half-naked woman on my shoulder.

"What's up, Mike?"

"Call Artra," I said. "Tell her to come to my place. Medical emergency."

I carried my strange cargo up to my unit. The key was under the clay turtle in the flower garden. I did a nice thigh-burning squat, keeping her positioned, got the key, stood and went up the steps with her. I unlocked the door, and just as I stepped in, she jerked.

And thunked her head on the door jamb.

She stopped moving again.

I LAID HER down on my sofa and got a blanket to cover her up. I checked her forehead and saw a little bump where she'd banged her head. I went to the fridge and got the ice tray from the freezer, ran it under some water and loosened a cube. I wrapped the cube in a napkin and went back to the sofa.

I smoothed away the hair from her face. She was beautiful in a natural way. She'd had some makeup on the night before. It was a little smeared and faded. She looked to be in her mid-twenties, but there were lines at the corners of her eyes that belonged to a much older person.

I gently put the ice on the bump on her head. She groaned a little. Her eyes were closed but her face was twisted, like little knots of pain were pulling tight inside her.

There was no use speculating on what had happened. It could've been a thousand different things. My guess was that the alcohol thing was it. Malibu is not generally known for its bibulous restraint.

So what about the lack of clothing? A love scene gone bad? Someone who had been with her while she was drinking—or drugging—herself. Her condition when I found her was such that she had to have come from one of the beach houses. Access to the sand is cut off all along PCH. She didn't wander down from the street.

She had to be a model or an actress. Her face and body made that the most likely story. Looking like she did, you don't get very far in this town without some agent or producer trying to make you a star. The problem is it could be as a porn star. Hollywood, they say, is the only town where you can die of encouragement.

There was a knock on my screen door. The doctor had arrived.

ARTRA MURRAY WORE a pink bathrobe and fuzzy blue slippers. But don't let that fool you. She's as tough as they come. Sixty-ish, she had been the first African-American woman head of surgery at Johns Hopkins. She left it all to become a missionary surgeon in Kenya, where she lived through ten years of epidemics and persecutions.

Now she was in a unit in Paradise Cove so she could run a free health clinic up the coast, near Pepperdine University.

"What have you got?" she said.

"See for yourself," I said.

"Where's your shirt?"

"On her."

"Uh-huh."

"It's not like that, Doctor."

"Uh-huh."

Artra stepped over to the sofa. She dropped to a knee and started feeling the woman's face, talking to me as she did.

"Where'd she come from?"

"The beach. I was running."

"Was she lying there?"

"No, staggering around."

Artra pulled back the woman's eyelids, started fingering her throat.

"She's vomited," Artra said.

She squeezed the woman's mouth open and leaned over. Then sniffed.

"Get a shirt on," Artra said. "We're taking her to emergency."

"What is it?"

"This girl's been poisoned."

I DRIVE A restored '67 Mustang convertible named Spinoza. It was given in lieu of a fee to Ira by one of his grateful clients. Ira is giving me a lease-option on it in return for my stellar investigatory services. Named for the Dutch philosopher whose radical views got him kicked out of his Jewish community. He became something of a loner in this world, but one who kept looking for truth. To this I could relate. The car is dark-green on the outside with a saddle-tan interior. A perfect blending, which is also a reflection of Baruch Spinoza's unified view of substance. When I explained this to Ira he said I needed to get out more.

Artra sat in the back with the woman. She had slipped a pair of my sweat pants on her before we left. As we drove, Artra called ahead, explaining what was coming to the emergency room.

The hospital was four miles away. When I pulled in,

there was a male nurse standing outside the doors with a wheelchair.

He helped Artra get our charge in the chair, wheeled her in. I parked the car and joined Artra at the desk. She was talking to the reception nurse, a woman, and said, "Here he is" when I got there.

I answered a few questions and Artra filled in with her medical opinion. Then we went into a small waiting room where CNN was showing with the sound muted. That's the best way to watch the news. We sat.

"So she was out there alone on the beach?" Artra said.

"Yep."

"Good thing you came along when you did."

"How bad is she?"

"Not good."

"What kind of poison is it?"

"Nicotine."

"Nicotine? What would deliver a lethal dose?"

"My first guess is insecticide."

"What a way to go," I said.

Artra said, "The question is, did somebody do it, or did she do it to herself?"

"And how'd she get out on the beach?"

Artra nodded. "She didn't say anything?"

"Only one word. But I didn't understand it. Sounded like *higog.*"

"Egg nog maybe?"

"Not really the season, is it?"

"I know some people who nog all the time," Artra said. "Never cared for it myself."

"Thanks for coming over," I said.

"It's what I do." She paused. "Mike, what do you do? I mean, when you're not chiseling that fine body?"

"Me? Chisel?"

"I see you doing push-ups out there on the sand."

"I like the sound of the ocean."

"Not a lot of money in that, is there?"

"I do some work for Ira," I said.

"Ah. He's a good man."

"I'd like to be half as good someday."

"What's stopping you?" she said.

"You sound like a head doctor now."

"Doesn't truth conquer all things?" She smiled. She'd correctly translated the Latin phrase tattooed on my left forearm.

"Nicely done," I said.

Then she looked at my left hand, which was resting on my knee. She picked it up softly, looked it over. "Your little finger," she said. "It was severed?"

I nodded. "But I've been digitally remastered."

"Wow," she said. "That's rare, especially considering the location of the laceration. You have good use of it?"

"It's coming back. It has PTSD. I don't want to rush it."

She laughed. "Now I really want to know about you, Mr. Mike Romeo."

"Someday, Doctor."

Part of me hoped that day would come. I'd fight it, but it would be nice to be able to trust someone else in this world. Besides Ira, that is.

A short time later a woman in blue scrubs came into the waiting room.

"Hello, Artra," she said.

Artra stood. "Good to see you, Gabriella."

They shook hands.

Artra said, "This is my friend, Mike Romeo. Mike, Dr. Gabriella Pedroza."

She had a good, strong grip and a warm smile. Late thirties.

"She's going to make it," Dr. Pedroza said. "We've

administered activated charcoal and her vitals are stable. We found traces of vomitus. That probably saved her life."

"Thank God," Artra said.

"How'd she get this way?" the doctor said.

"We don't know."

"What's her name?"

"Again, don't know. Mike found her on the beach, alone."

Dr. Pedroza turned to me. "No ID?"

I shook my head.

"Probably a suicide attempt," Dr. Pedroza said. "You don't get that amount accidentally."

"Maybe not," I said.

The doctor looked at me. "Your reason?"

"She was out staggering around. If she wanted to kill herself, why would she do that? Also, she was stark naked."

Dr. Pedroza frowned. "How does that apply?"

"Women who commit suicide are usually dressed. They want the police to find them presentable. Men, who usually shoot themselves, don't care what they look like."

"How do you know all this?" she said.

"I read," I said.

"Impressive," she said.

"Can I come back and see her?" I said.

"Tomorrow morning," Dr. Pedroza said. "If you'd like to leave your number I can make sure you're notified."

"I'll be here," I said.

"So will I," Dr. Pedroza said.

"YOU MADE AN impression on Gabriella," Artra said. We were driving back to the Cove.

"How so?" I said.

"A woman can tell. Are you involved with anyone, Mike?"

"Not at the moment."

"Interested in anyone?"

"You're moving out of your field, Doctor," I said.

"Just friendly conversation," she said.

I tapped my thumbs on Spinoza's steering wheel.

"A conversation usually means two sides," Artra said.

"Okay," I said. "I am interested in someone."

"Do tell."

"Plotinus."

"Excuse me?"

"The philosopher. He had this idea that we can't know ultimate truth through language and rationality, only by uniting with the Absolute."

A long silence followed.

Finally, Artra said, "You are an interesting guy, Mike."

"That's one word for it."

When we got to the Cove, Artra asked me if I'd like some coffee. I thanked her, but told her I wanted to get back to the beach before too many people got there. She said she understood. I wasn't sure if she did.

Rodney saw me walking by.

"So what happened?" he asked.

"She's going to be okay," I said. "We got her to the hospital in time."

He looked relieved. "The cops came around."

"Did you talk to them?"

"They asked if I'd seen a big strong guy with a naked girl over his shoulder. I told 'em no."

"But you did see me."

"The girl had a T-shirt on. So she was only half-naked."

"Rodney…"

"Far as I'm concerned, what happens in the Cove stays in the Cove. I don't want you getting in trouble."

"Ditto, Rodney. If they come back send them down to the beach."

When I got down to the sand, most of the fog had gone and I thought about finishing my run.

Instead, I sat and just listened to the waves.

There's something about that sound that makes me think things can be reborn. Even somebody who can't seem forget the people he's killed.

Somebody said, "Hey, man."

IT WAS A guy I'd seen around the Cove. Maybe mid-twenties. Long, curly blond hair flopping around like an overturned bowl of fusilli pasta. Scrawny. I could have put my thumb and index finger around his wrist and still had room for a couple of pencils and a Swiss Army knife.

"Hey man yourself," I said.

He dropped to the sand next to me. He wore only red-and-black board shorts. He looked like a fence post with Christmas wrapping. He held a glass pipe, a Bic lighter, and a small baggie of combustible weed.

"Join me?" he said.

"I only walk on grass," I said.

"Cool with me." He packed his pipe and fired it up. He held in the smoke, his head nodding slightly, before letting it out.

"You a dawn to dusk man?" I said.

"Huh?"

"Bake all day?"

"So?"

"Ever think of resting your brain?"

"Huh?"

"So it functions optimally."

"Opt ... I don't get what you're saying, man."

"My point," I said.

He shrugged and looked at the ocean.

"What's your name?" I said.

"Call me C Dog."

"A dog of the sea?"

"No, man. C, like in my first name, which is Carter, which I hate."

"Call me Mike," I said.

He nodded and fired up another hit.

"What do you do, C?" I said. "I mean, when you're not raising your consciousness."

"My what?"

"Your work, what do you do?"

"I got a band," he said. "Unopened Cheese."

I blinked a couple of times.

"Like it?" he said.

"It's got a certain aroma," I said.

"A what?"

"Makes you stop and think. It's always good to stop every now and then and think, don't you think?"

His brow furrowed as the question trudged through the mud of his synapses.

"I guess so, man," he said finally. "What do you think about?"

I picked up a fistful of sand in my right hand and let it slowly run out. "Whether there's ultimate truth, or whether we're just accidents of blind materialistic forces."

C Dog sat silent, eyes unmoving for a long time. Then he made a *whoosh* sound and ran his hand over his head.

Whoosh indeed, C Dog. That sound may sum up all our attempts to make sense of existence. At least you have a band. Make music, my friend.

"You look like you can fight," C Dog said.

"I don't like violence," I said.

"I'm gonna take some MMA."

"Yeah?"

"Somebody mouths off, I want to shut his face and make him hurt."

I shook my head. "That's not the way. Not the way at all."

"Huh?"

"The *way*. It is *not*."

"What's the way, man?"

"You don't find meaning through the physical dominance of another, just because of a verbal insult."

C Dog's mouth was now hanging open. His red-rimmed eyes blinked twice, lingeringly, as if trying to focus.

Then he said, "You talk kind of weird, man."

I didn't argue.

"But I kind of like it," he said. "You wanna come over sometime and shotgun some brew and we can talk more?"

"We will talk of many things," I said.

He prepped another bowl.

A WOMAN AND a little boy had come down to the beach. The woman looked like the grandmother. She held the boy's hand as they tested the water with their feet.

The boy giggled.

That was a nice sound.

It was interrupted by three guys and three girls who ran down from the parking lot to the beach. They had beers and a football and beach bodies and weren't shy about showing them off.

A couple of the guys upped the volume on their laughter and observations of the world. These observations married the word *Mother* with another word that started with an *F*. This began a cycle that fed on itself. The word led to laughter, and the laughter to more of the word.

The grandmother with the little boy looked at the guys.

I got up and walked over to the group.

"Greetings," I said.

They looked at me. One of them, the biggest one, was about my size. Obviously pushed weights. He had an iron-mail tattoo that covered the upper left quadrant of his chest and went down his left arm to the elbow. Looked like the fighting sleeve on Spartacus.

"You guys from around here?" I said.

"What's up?" the big one said.

I said, "We have families come down here, so I thought maybe you could watch the language a little."

The others in the group looked at the big guy to see what he'd do. He was clearly the Moe of these stooges, the unofficial leader.

"We're just hangin', man, it's a public beach," Spartacus said.

"Right on," I said. "Just thought you could tone it down."

"Sure, sure," he said. Then smiled. Then added, in a loud voice, that it was a good effing idea.

He did not use the word *effing*.

Gales of laughter from the others.

"All right," I said "You made your point. How about, as a favor to me, a resident of these shores, you refrain from the harsher language choices when children are near."

"Man, you talk funny." He took a step toward me. "Like you're backassing me."

"Far be it from me to do that, friend," I said. "If anything, I'm frontassing. If that's anatomically possible."

Sparty did a grab-hand on his crotch.

"Is that necessary?" I said.

Sparty smiled. Then turned his back and said he wanted to play some more mothereffing football.

I tapped him on the shoulder.

He whipped around with a right cross aimed at my jaw. I ducked it and stepped back.

"Whoa, hold off there, Lightning," I said. "That's not the way."

"Get outta here," Sparty said, "or you'll get more of the same."

"You mean missing me with a punch?"

One of the other stooges spoke up. He was a little leaner than Sparty. "Dude, he's a third-degree black belt in Karate. You don't want to mess with him."

"Really?" I said. "Third degree?"

Sparty smiled.

"That's a fine achievement," I said. "You do know that *kara* is an ancient word that means to cleanse oneself of evil thoughts, and to be humbly receptive to peace and gentleness. Yes? You are therefore abusing your own discipline. That's not a good way to live—"

"Shut it!"

"You see?"

"Last warning," he said.

"You don't intend to smooth out your tongue?" I said.

He made with the F-bomb again.

I turned and walked toward the water.

Sparty and his friends laughed and tossed some insults at my back, peppered with the language I had requested they eschew.

Where the water met the sand was a dump of wet kelp. The amber-colored tangle had a healthy crop of bulbs. I found one the size of large egg and pulled it off and stuck it in the pocket of my shorts.

The boys were tossing the football. Sparty's back was to me. One of others warned him I was coming.

Sparty, football in hand, turned.

And threw the ball as hard as he could at me.

It hit my abs and I cradled it with my left hand. A nice catch, I must say.

I turned and threw the football into the water.

Now it was about saving face. Sparty couldn't afford to be cleansed or humbled in front of the ladies and the stooges.

He came at me and decided to lead with his left foot.

It was awful. If this guy was third-degree black belt in any form of Karate I was the world's greatest living philosopher.

I grabbed his leg under my arm and gave him four iron fingers to the throat.

He hit the sand like a little girl's doll, his eyes wide and his mouth open as he gasped for air.

I took out the seaweed bulb and shoved it in his mouth. He was going to have some fun breathing now.

The shock to the stooges must have been real, because not one of them moved.

Sparty made horrible gasping sounds. His face reddened nicely.

"Anyone else?" I said.

"Damn, man!" the lean one said. "He's hurt!"

I raised my finger. "What did I say about the language?"

He stopped talking.

"Now," I said, "I'm going to suggest you all go find another beach."

Spartacus wheezed, coughed. The bulb came out of his mouth. I shoved it back in and closed his mouth by shoving his chin.

"Get him out of here," I said.

I backed away as the group came to him and helped him up. He spat the bulb out and coughed. As they made their way to the parking lot one of the girls gave me the finger.

Who says people don't communicate anymore?

I decided then I needed a swim to wash off the stink of my latest encounter. I'd almost forgotten about the grand-mother and the boy. Just before I took to the surf she walked toward me.

"God bless you," she said.

The boy was looking at me curiously. I put out my hand. He gave me five.

A blessing and a five.

I figured that was the best I could do for the morning.

C Dog was still sitting where I'd left him. "Man, that was so cool."

"Nothing cool about it," I said.

"Oh, man!" His big, dopey grin got on my nerves.

"I'll see you," I said, and ran into the ocean. I dove at a wave, feeling the cool crispness of the Pacific in November. I thought of Ishmael then, at the beginning of *Moby-Dick*. He said he suffered from a *damp, drizzly November* in his soul and his answer was to put out to sea.

He took a boat.

I swam.

At least I didn't run into any whales.

NEXT MORNING I went back to the hospital to see about my mermaid. I checked in at the desk. The receptionist ran her finger along a clipboard, nodded.

"I have your name," she said and handed me a visitor badge.

It was nice knowing someone had my name.

"You'll find her in Room 210," the receptionist said. I took the elevator to the second floor and walked a short distance to Room 210. The door was open.

Hospital rooms all smell the same to me. A mix of antiseptic cleaning agent and human frailty. This one was no different. The human frailty was sitting on an incline in one of the two beds.

She looked halfway normal now. Her hair was brushed and her eyes clear.

"Hello," I said.

"Are you the one who found me?" she said.

"I am."

"Thank you."

"How you feeling?"

"Okay," she said. She pinched her hospital gown between her thumb and forefinger. "I didn't have any clothes on, did I?"

"I put my T-shirt on you. I hope you don't mind. I wasn't sweating yet."

She glanced past me as if trying to see if anyone was listening. "Does anybody know I'm here?" she said.

"Well," I said, "there's me and Dr. Murray and the staff here."

"Who's Dr. Murray?"

"She's a friend, lives in Paradise Cove. She's the one who figured out you had poison in you."

She closed her eyes.

I said, "Is there somebody we can contact?"

"Please just get me out of here."

"Where will you go?"

"I have friends."

"How'd you get poisoned?"

She turned her head away.

I slid a chair over and sat. "Why don't you try to tell me what happened. Maybe I can help."

"No," she said quickly, turning to look at me. Then thought a moment. "Why would you want to try, anyway? You don't know me."

"I carried you into my home," I said. "I figure we are acquainted."

"Can you just get me out of here?"

"Would it help if I told you that you can trust me?"

She shook her head.

"Can I at least know your name?" I said.

"I'd rather not."

"Okay," I said. "But you can call me Mike."

A voice behind me said, "And you both can call me Deputy Stevens."

THE WOMAN TENSED.

I stood to face the cop. He was average height, blond-haired. He could have stepped right off the beach and into the county sheriff's uniform he wore. He eyed me coolly.

"Morning," I said.

He nodded. "I understand there was a possible homicide attempt."

"Please make him go away!" the woman said.

"Ma'am?" the deputy said.

"I don't want to talk to anybody!"

"I'm here to help you."

"No! I won't say anything!"

"Ma'am, if you'll just—" He started to go around me.

I slid in front of him. "Maybe this isn't the right time."

"Who are you, anyway?" he said.

"A friend."

"Well, friend, you can leave the room now."

"No," the woman said.

"She'd rather not talk," I said.

"Back off, please."

"Now look, Deputy Stevens, she doesn't have to talk to you. She's not a suspect."

"She's a victim."

"No, I'm not!" she said.

"There you go," I said.

"I'm going to find out what happened to her," Deputy Stevens said.

"Only if she voluntarily chooses to talk," I said. "She can refuse."

"You a lawyer?"

"I work for a lawyer."

Deputy Stevens's brain started chugging. "You can talk to me voluntarily, ma'am. There's no reason you wouldn't want to do that, is there?"

"That's a very clever question," I said. "Socratic."

He blinked. "What did you just say to me?"

"Socratic."

He looked me up and down.

"You the boyfriend?" he said. "Maybe you did it."

"No!" the woman said.

He looked over my shoulder. "Ma'am, may I speak to you?"

"I don't want to," she said in almost a whisper.

"I guess that's it," I said.

He looked at me again. "You live around here?"

"Close by."

"Where?"

"I don't see the relevance of that question. Socrates would tell you—"

"This is a small town," Deputy Stevens said. "You better remember that."

"Your card would remind me," I said.

He angry-frowned at me as he fished out a card.

"I'll let you know if she changes her mind," I said.

"I won't," she said.

Deputy Stevens took a step back, gave us each one more lawman's stare, then left.

"Are we going to get in trouble?" the woman said.

"I'm always in trouble," I said. "You're fine. But why don't you want to talk to him? Is it because somebody tried to kill you, and you're afraid of this person?"

Her face matched the sheet. "Please, just get me out of here."

"This isn't a prison. I'll go talk to the doctor. But can I at least know your name?"

She looked at me and for the first time I saw warmth in her eyes.

"Okay," she said. "Brooklyn."

DR. GABRIELLA PEDROZA met me at the nurse's station.

"Nice to see you again," she said.

"Can she leave now?" I said.

"With you?"

I nodded.

"Certainly, if that's what she wants," she said. "I'll give you some instructions for her."

"Thanks, Doc."

"You're the one who should be thanked. You saved her life." She paused. "If you want to let me know how she's doing, you can always leave me a message here. I'll return your call."

I shook her hand.

It was a little after nine when I walked Brooklyn outside and into the sun. No fog this morning. Brooklyn was back in my T-shirt and sweat pants and hospital-issued slippers. She kicked off the slippers and tossed them into a trash bin.

"I prefer bare feet," she said.

We got in Spinoza and I said, "Where can I take you?"

"Kahuna's," she said.

Kahuna's is a local restaurant and bar on PCH. They serve killer *huevos rancheros*.

"You want breakfast?" I said.

"Yes!"

"Can I buy?"

KAHUNA'S LOOKS LIKE a Polynesian beach hut on steroids, with twin gables adorned by fake thatched-palm leaves. Calls to mind the romance of the South Seas or another clever L.A. cover job, like a Beverly Hills toupee.

The young hostess, dressed in a floral-print sarong, greeted Brooklyn by name. She showed us to a table by the window looking out at the ocean, just as a pelican glided along the surface looking for his own breakfast.

"I wish I could fly," Brooklyn said.

The pelican didn't find anything, made a big U-turn in the air, came back.

"It won't be long now," she said.

"What won't be?" I said.

"Everything will be all right now." She said it as if trying to convince herself.

A waitress came to the table. Brooklyn ordered Earl Grey tea and steel-cut oatmeal. I asked for coffee and the aforementioned *huevos rancheros.*

Our pelican was still coming up with bupkis.

"What's it say on your arm?" Brooklyn said.

"*Vincit Omnia Veritas,*" I said. "Latin for truth conquers all things."

"Uck," she said.

"Uck?"

"Conquer. I don't like that word."

"No?"

"We have too much killing in the world."

"Truth doesn't want to kill you. It wants to set you free."

"That's not funny."

"I wasn't being funny."

She leaned forward, giving me a serious look. "Earth is about to be reborn."

"It could use it," I said.

"It's true. Michael has spoken."

For a second, I thought she meant me.

"The angel," she said.

Ruled me out.

"The archangel from the Bible?" I said.

"He's real. He speaks through chosen people. That's how I know Earth is going to be reborn. He's returning to Earth."

The waitress came back with our drinks. The coffee was good and strong. Brooklyn unpackaged her tea bag, laid it in the cup, then poured the hot water in.

"Can I ask you something?" I said.

"Uh-huh."

"When I picked you up on the beach, you said something. You were obviously out of it, but it sounded like *higog.*"

She stared at me. Like she was trying to remember.

"I'm sorry," she said.

"No worries," I said.

She looked out the window. "Look at her. Isn't she beautiful?"

"The ocean?"

"And all we do is hurt her. In hurting her, we are hurting ourselves. We have a collective soul and we damage it and then we turn on ourselves."

She looked back at me. "Does that make sense?"

"Maybe people are just messed up. All world religions and philosophies recognize that. People are just a roiling mass of conflict."

"But what makes them that way?"

"It's the big question, isn't it? Why are we the way we are? What can we do about it? Do we even care about doing anything about it?"

"That's why we have to get back to Earth," she said. "Earth is the only thing that matters, the only thing nurtures us and lasts."

"How did that poison get inside you, Brooklyn?"

It was as if I'd slapped her. She reeled back in her chair. "Stop it. Don't ask me that."

"You had a lot of nasty stuff in your stomach."

"It doesn't matter."

"I don't want to see it happen to you again."

"It won't."

"How can you—"

"Please stop."

We sat in silence for a long time. I kept watching for our pelican friend. But he'd moved on.

The waitress brought our food. Brooklyn's oatmeal came with little serving dishes of raisins, walnuts, and brown sugar. She poured the contents of each into the bowl and stirred it with her spoon. She then took up a healthy spoonful and blissfully savored it.

I kept the conversation light as we ate. We talked about how she got her name—her grandfather was a fan of the Dodgers when they played at Ebbets Field—and where she grew up (Montclair, New Jersey) and what her favorite movies were (*Lord of the Rings* and *Shrek*). But when I probed about her coming out to L.A., she clammed.

And turned things back on me, wanting to know where I grew up and where I went to college.

I deflected. Only Ira knows my story and I'm keeping it that way.

She asked if I did any fighting. People ask me that all the time. Must be my charm. I told her I did a little cage fighting once but got smart and quit.

We were about finished when a man the size of Samoa rumbled to our table. He was definitely Pacific Islander, wearing a Talofa shirt of ocean blue which was the male attire at Kahuna's.

The giant gave me the stink eye.

"Kalolo!" Brooklyn said.

He looked at her. "You okay?"

She nodded. "Kalolo, this is Mike."

I put my hand out. He ignored it.

His arms were like sewer pipes. His left forearm had a tat, in roughly the same place I had mine. Only his was a bared-teeth bulldog wearing a Smokey Bear hat with the United States Marine Corps emblem on it. Underneath were the letters *USMC.*

"Uncle Sam's Misguided Children," I said.

"You ex?" Kalolo said.

I shook my head.

"Then it's not funny," he said. He looked at Brooklyn. "I'll be at the bar."

She nodded.

Samoa stomped away.

"Charming," I said.

"He's a good man," Brooklyn said.

"Is he why you think everything's all right?"

"Thank you for helping me," she said. "I'm going to be okay now."

It sounded like she believed it. Which is usually how abuse victims end up back in the hospital—or the morgue.

"I wish you'd let me keep in touch," I said.

"Thank you for breakfast," she said. She got up and held out her hand. I took it. "And for being such a nice guy."

I paid the bill in cash. As I walked out, I saw Brooklyn seated at the bar talking to Kalolo. He was pointing his finger at her. She was shaking her head.

FOUR DAYS LATER, a Tuesday, it was time for my regularly scheduled meet-up with Ira Rosen.

Ira is a rabbi, lawyer, and former Mossad agent who looks like your favorite uncle. Acts and sounds like him, too, unless you try to hurt someone he knows. He's a paraplegic, the result of a firefight in Beirut. His head, though, is the most impressive part of him. What's inside it, I mean.

"You haven't exactly been the model of communication," Ira said, pouring me some of his tea concoction. I usually associate tea drinking with flowered hats and white gloves. Ira Rosen has tried to disabuse me of that notion.

We were seated in the living room of his Los Feliz home. Floor-to-ceiling bookshelves dominated the décor. Books on law and philosophy and religion mingled with great works of literature and history and military science. Ira was a university on wheels and a man of spiritual serenity. He'd taken me in when I first got to L.A. I'd managed to attract a Dumpster-load of trouble since then, but Ira apparently accepts that as part of the hazardous duty of being my friend and sometime employer.

"Nothing going on," I said. "The beach is so dull."

Ira studied my face. He can read me like a racing form. "Oh?"

"Like the other day," I said. "I'm running along the beach like I always do, and a naked woman stumbles toward me."

"Ha, ha," Ira said.

"She'd been poisoned."

"Better and better."

"I called Artra, and we got her to the hospital."

"Wait a minute. You're serious?"

I took a sip of tea. Winced.

"Michael, talk to me."

"The tea is delightful," I said, putting the cup on the table so I wouldn't have to touch it again.

"Michael ..."

"The young lady is all right," I said. "Though she refuses to tell me how it happened."

Ira shook his head. "Dullsville at the beach, eh?"

"Totally," I said. "Except for a little scuffle."

Ira clacked his tea cup on the saucer, like a judge banging a gavel. "Don't tell me."

"Okay," I said.

"No, tell me."

"It wasn't really much," I said. "Guy was using foul language in the presence of a little boy and his grandmother."

"And you did what?"

"Tried to reason with him."

"Oh no."

"He was not the reasonable type."

"Did it get physical?"

"Define physical."

"Maybe I'll just show you."

"I didn't want to get into it," I said. "Really. But the guy wouldn't stop."

"So you did what?"

"Slowed him down."

"How?"

"With a love tap."

"You're going to get yourself arrested, you know. And good old Ira is not going to come around with bail."

"He deserved it," I said.

"What, exactly?"

"I kinked his windpipe."

"That could have killed him."

I stood. "It didn't."

"Was the little boy watching?"

"What?"

"The little boy you mentioned. Did he see that?"

"I don't know. I guess so."

"Did you think about what that might do to him?"

"No."

"Then who was being unreasonable?"

I hate the way Ira can nail me. But I wasn't in a mood to be nailed.

"Maybe it's time he learned," I said. "Maybe it was the best thing that could have happened to him."

"To see you fight a guy and hurt him like that?"

"Exactly that. Best that he knows what the world is like."

"And to act like you?"

"Sure."

"Your inner Achilles," Ira said. "I thought you didn't trust him."

"So I was wrong." I made a grand motion toward the books surrounding us. "What's the big lesson of history, Ira? It's all about power, dominance. You fight and win, or you don't fight and lose. Rage keeps us alive. Civility is overrated."

"You don't believe that, Michael."

"And why don't you stop telling me what I believe?"

"There's an old story," Ira said.

"With you there always is," I said.

"Shut up and listen."

"Is that any way for a rabbi to talk?"

"When dealing with a smarty-pants, a hot iron is called for."

"Continue," I said.

"There was a boy walking along a beach one day. On the sand were starfish, as far as the eye could see. They'd been washed up and were now baking in the sun. He saw an old man pick up one of the starfish and hurl it back into the sea. Then he did it again. The boy approached and said, to the man, 'Why are you bothering to do that, sir? There are too many. What you are doing will make no difference.' The old man smiled, picked up another starfish, and returned it to the ocean. 'It makes a difference to that one,' he said."

"That's sweet," I said. "And doomed to failure."

"If we all thought that—"

34

"The world's full of cockroaches, not starfish. If we have the chance to smash one, we do it. We put off the inevitable a little while."

I stood.

"Come on, finish your tea," Ira said. "Let's talk of—"

"And no more watered-down leaves, Ira. I don't ever want to drink tea again, yours or anybody else's."

"Take a breath."

"I will," I said. "Outside."

Achilles and I left by the front door.

I KEPT WALKING till I hit Vermont. Headed over to the Argo, a used bookstore. Bookstores always calm me down.

I told myself that was the only reason I was going inside.

But I knew I was full of it.

There was another reason.

Her name was Sophie.

Ever since I'd bought some books a while back, she'd make an occasional appearance in my thoughts. As if to taunt me with a dream of normalcy.

A dream I don't have very often.

She was there, behind the counter. Tall, athletic form, with long hair the color of red oak leaves in autumn. Intelligent eyes behind black-framed glasses.

She was jotting something in a journal of some kind. She didn't see me as I walked up.

"Any first edition Rabelais?" I said.

She looked up. Smiled. "Well, hello. Haven't seen you for a while."

She'd noticed.

"I moved," I said. "But I miss the old neighborhood."

Maybe more than I wanted to admit.

"Can I help you find anything?" she said.

A place of peace, a spirit of repose, a way not to hurt people. I'll take one of those, Sophie. Thanks.

"No first edition Rabelais?" I said.

"We're fresh out," she said. "But I expect a whole shipment next week."

"Put one aside for me," I said.

A customer came to the counter with a stack of books, so I went browsing. In the literature section I found a paperback of *Moby-Dick* with the Rockwell Kent illustrations. My father had a hardback edition of same, which haunted me as a kid. The etching of Ahab on deck, with his peg leg and long coat, the wind at his face, his beady eyes looking out over his sharp nose at the cold sea where the white whale lived.

He looked like a man trapped inside himself, driven by demons he couldn't suppress.

Even then, as a boy in a blubbery body always getting picked on, I thought I understood Ahab.

But also Ishmael.

I took the used copy of *Moby-Dick* to one of the sofas the Argo provides for its customers and opened to chapter one again. *Call me Ishmael,* he says. Then he talks about finding himself *pausing before coffin warehouses, and bringing up the rear of every funeral I meet.* And it's everything he can do to keep himself from *deliberately stepping into the street, and methodically knocking people's hats off.*

When he's like that, he goes to sea. It's his *substitute for pistol and ball.*

What was my substitute?

I dipped into it a little more. I re-read my favorite chapter, *The Lee Shore,* dedicated to the helmsman, Bulkington. It ends, *Up from the spray of thy ocean-perishing—straight up, leaps thy apotheosis!*

That did it. I put the book back on the shelf and walked out to the counter.

Sophie had just finished with a customer.

"Find anything?" she asked.

"My apotheosis."

"Excuse me?"

"Sorry. I was reading *Moby-Dick*. I meant lunch."

She cocked her head.

"Would you consider having lunch with me?" I said.

"Wow," she said "I'm ..."

"Flummoxed?"

"Not the word I was looking for, but yes."

"It was worth a shot," I said.

"It was. So yes."

"Yes?"

"Yes."

"Okay."

What a conversationalist I had become. I should have a talk show.

"How about lunch on Thursday?" she said.

Feeling like the schoolboy I had once been, I said, "Shall I pick you up?"

"Why don't we meet? Do you know Hammett's? On Hyperion?"

"I'll find it," I said.

"Noon?"

"Perfect," I said. And it was.

For that moment at least.

WHEN I GOT back to my mobile home there was a Ford pickup jutting out of my driveway. We don't have much space here in the Cove. Spinoza takes up three quarters of the space. So I had to park him crossways behind the pickup. This did not make me happy.

As soon as I walked through my little gate, I saw a man sitting on the deck chair on my porch.

He stood up. He was in his fifties, portly, wore a short-sleeve shirt untucked over khaki trousers. His arms were hairy and tan. He looked like a man who worked with his hands.

"Your truck is in my driveway," I said.

"Are you Mike?" His voice was strained. But it was his eyes that got me. Pleading.

"This is my place," I said.

"May I talk with you for a moment?"

"What about?"

"Brooklyn," he said.

"What about Brooklyn?"

"She's my daughter," he said. "She's missing."

"Come inside," I said.

He sat on the same sofa where I had put Brooklyn's inert body five days earlier. I asked if he wanted anything to drink and he said no. I pulled up a chair and sat across from him.

"You're the one who saved her life?" he said.

"I happened to be in the right place at the right time. My friend, a doctor, drove her to the hospital."

"Someone tried to kill her," he said.

"Do you know that for sure?"

"Not for sure, but I know it just the same."

"Brooklyn didn't tell me your name."

"Ray. Ray Christie."

I nodded. "Can I ask how you happened to find me?"

"Brooklyn called me. Let's see, on Friday. She told me what happened, told me about you finding her. That you lived in Paradise Cove. I told the fellow at the gate I was looking for you, that the girl you found on the beach was my daughter. He questioned me, made me describe her, show my I.D., which is his job, I guess."

"Mine too," I said. "Can I see your I.D., please?"

"Yeah, yeah." He took his wallet from his back pocket and got out his license, handed it to me.

"You're from Prescott?" I said.

"That's right," he said.

"What do you do there?"

"I have a drywall business."

I gave him back the license.

I said, "What time did she call you on Friday?"

"Afternoon. It was strange."

"Strange how?"

"We hadn't talked in five years."

He paused, took a deep breath. Looked at the floor and shook his head a little.

"I was so glad to hear from her," Ray Christie said. "I lost my wife, you see and ..." His eyes were reddening. I got up and went to the bathroom and got a box of Kleenex. I came back and put the box on the coffee table and sat back down, waiting for him to continue.

He took a tissue and dabbed at his eyes. "I'm sorry, I shouldn't be like this."

"No worries," I said.

He took in a long breath. "She wanted to reconcile, I'm sure of it. But then she said she had to go and would call me back. She never did."

"Did you try calling her?"

"I don't have her number."

"It should be on your phone's log. You have it?"

"I have a land line at home. That's how she called me."

"When did you get to L.A.?"

"Yesterday. I went to the police, but I know they just stick these things in the system and nothing happens. That's when I thought of coming to you, Mr. Romeo."

"Why was that?" I said.

"Brooklyn spoke highly of you. That you protected her from a policeman. That you were some sort of investigator?"

"I do my investigations for a lawyer, when he has a client."

"I just thought I'd take a shot."

I said, "Have you considered that she might not want to be found?"

"Meaning what?"

"Maybe she ran off with someone. Maybe she decided to go to Vegas. Maybe she changed her mind on a moment's notice about seeing you."

He shook his head hard. "No. No way. That wasn't in her voice."

"I'm talking about what's in her head," I said.

Ray Christie let out a sigh that was almost like he'd been punched in the gut. "Isn't there any way you can help me?"

"Technically, no," I said.

"I can pay you," he said. Desperation in his voice.

And suddenly I thought of starfish.

"Tell me more about Brooklyn," I said.

RAY CHRISTIE'S EYES got a far-off look. "When she was little, we were close. After her mother died ... You know how hard that is?"

I nodded. When your parents are murdered, you kind of get to know how hard it is.

"Kelly, my wife, she was the one who knew what was going on, what to do with a girl. I always did what she said. When she died, I had to try to learn all that on the fly. I grew up in a family of three boys. I knew nothing about raising a daughter. I still don't, I guess."

He took another Kleenex.

"My sister-in-law tried to help me, but she lives in St. Louis and most of the time it was over the phone. I felt help-less. Then Brooklyn started to change."

"In what way?"

"Her whole demeanor. As I think back on it, it was like it

happened overnight. One day she was the daughter I had known all those years, and the next she was a different person. She didn't laugh as much. She got more serious. Quieter. I figured she was going through whatever high school kids go through. I even tried to talk to her about it all, but she just denied that anything was different. But it was. I could feel it as much as a breeze in the trees."

"So no theory on why she changed?"

He didn't answer right away. He took in a deep breath, let it out audibly. "I have a theory all right. But it's too late to do anything about it."

I waited for him to go on.

"She had a friend. A close friend from high school. Celia. Red-haired girl who hardly ever smiled. Anyway, Brooklyn used to spend a lot of time with her, slept over at her house and things like that. Celia's father was a union electrician, worked for the studios. He was always nice to me. The mother seemed a little ... strained."

"Strained?"

"Nervous. Anxious. Stressed out. She had four kids pretty close in age. I got the impression she was the one who did all the looking after. And wasn't too pleased about that."

"Mothers have no union," I said.

He nodded. "So anyway, this family moves away about a year after this change I've been talking about. I asked Brooklyn if she missed Celia, and she shrugged and said, 'I guess.' That's a strange thing to say about your best friend, don't you think?"

"I do."

"Well, this goes on like this, up through high school. I'm not saying we had bad times together, Brooklyn and me. It's just that we were never as close. That hurt more than I ..."

He stopped, choked up. Cleared his throat. "About three years ago, I come around a grocery aisle and almost run into Celia's mom. She'd put on a lot of weight, but I knew her right away. And she knew me. I said hello and she said hello and I asked her about Celia, and she said Celia was managing a Starbucks in Tucson. I asked how her husband, Bernie was his name, how he was doing, and her face tightened up. 'We got divorced,' she said. 'Oh,' I said. 'I'm sorry.' 'I'm not,' she said. Then she said she was in a rush and told me to give her best to Brooklyn and was off like a greyhound chasing a mechanical rabbit. It was strange."

"How?"

"Like she was afraid I was going to ask her another question. I'm not a suspicious person by nature, I like to think the best of everybody, but that knocked me back a couple of steps. It triggered all those feelings that I had when Brooklyn changed. So I went home and did a little digging on the internet. I did a search for Bernie's name, then changed the search to Bernard. And that's when I found it."

He paused, like he needed to gather strength.

"He'd died in jail. Got knifed. Or shanked, I guess they call it. Can you guess why?"

"Pedophile," I said.

"How'd you know?"

"Everything you've said to this point. Your theory is that this Bernie molested your daughter."

Ray Christie began to cry. I let him. He needed to get it out. He grabbed another tissue and controlled himself after about half a minute.

"Where are you staying, Mr. Christie?"

"I'm at a Motel 6 in Van Nuys."

"How do I get in touch with you?"

"I do have a cell phone." He leaned over so he could pull it out of his pants pocket. He held it up as if to prove he was member of the twenty-first century.

He gave me the number.

"Will you help me?" he said.

"There may not be much to help on," I said. "Like I said, Brooklyn could be anywhere, and perfectly happy."

"I just have a bad feeling. Anything you can do ..."

I thought it over.

"Maybe a little," I said. "I'll have to clear this with my lawyer boss."

"Will he let you?"

"I think I can talk him into it. We'll have to do a little background check on you."

"I understand. I'll pay you whatever you need."

"We can discuss that later," I said.

"Then you'll do it?" he said.

"I will."

"God bless you," he said.

My second blessing in less than a week.

I was on a roll.

THERE ARE THINGS that happen in L.A. that don't happen anywhere else.

Other cities have their vibes. San Francisco is the Roman god Bacchus on a bender. New York sticks out its chin. Chicago has big shoulders, cool jazz, and dead people who vote.

But Los Angeles is a place that just has more. Of everything. Including causes. Which is why I wasn't surprised at the light-duty trucks that rolled by my place after Ray Christie left.

Two guys carrying some rigging followed on foot.

"What's going on?" I asked.

"Rally," one of the guys said. "Save the earth kind of crap."

The other guy laughed.

The first guy took a folded piece of paper out of his back pocket and handed it to me.

"Keep it," he said. "But don't litter with it."
I unfolded the paper. It was a flyer:

Save Our Beaches!

Vote for Allison Ursula Serret for County Supervisor!

Allison is the only candidate who will stand against the further erosion of our precious beaches!

Tonight, come rally for the Earth and hear Allison Ursual Serret and Dr. Gary Pasfield in conversation.

Free Nachos!

On the flyer were photographs of Serret and this guy Pasfield. They were smiling like car salesmen during November clearance.

I CALLED IRA on the whitelisted phone he'd prepped for me. No data storage. No incoming numbers but what I allow. No GPS. Routed through a system in Israel.

"I got a job," I said.

"Slinging hash?" Ira said.

"What's wrong with slinging hash?"

"Did I say anything was wrong with it? Quite the contrary, it will keep you out of trouble. But somehow I don't think that's the job."

"I'm helping someone find his missing daughter."

Pause. "And this man is paying you?"

"A fair exchange for services rendered."

"What do you know about finding missing persons?"

"Remember Joey Feint?"

"Ah, the phantom detective you were apprenticed to."

"I retained all his valuable information," I said. "And I did some pretty good work up in San Francisco for you and Samuel Johnson."

"Granted. But bones were broken."

"You can't make an omelet if you don't crack some eggs."

"You are not licensed to do this kind of work."

I said, "You can figure something out."

"Oh, can I?"

"You always do. Like, if he's your client. That'll work."

"Who is he?"

"His name is Ray Christie. He's the father of that woman on the beach. Remember?"

"She's gone missing?"

"Apparently," I said.

"Why are you doing this, Michael?"

"I need to make some money."

"What's the real reason?"

He knows me too well. "It's about time I became a productive citizen," I said.

"Now that's the best news—"

"I may be needing your services," I said. "You know, all that computer stuff you're so good at."

"I am not signing off on this until—"

"Start with the girl. Her name is Brooklyn Christie. C-H-R-I-S-T-I-E. Get everything you can on her."

"Oh, just everything? Listen—"

"Have I told you lately that I love you?"

"Write me a sonnet," Ira said.

"I shall compare thee to a summer's sunburn," I said. "Good-bye, Ira."

"Wait."

"What?"

"Michael, that guy you met on the street, who knew you from back east. Jason Pratt?"

"What about him?"

"He's trying to smoke you out again," Ira said.

A while back Jason Pratt spotted me in downtown L.A. He was a bully from my prep school days. He knew me as Michael Chamberlain, and that the New Haven cops wanted to talk to me about a dead man. The dead man happened to be somebody mixed up with the shooting deaths of my parents. Yes, he was dead. And yes, I had done it.

Pratt found me and wanted money to keep the story to himself. I responded in my usual gentle manner, by pushing him up against a wall and threatening him.

It didn't work. He became the source of an internet story that asked if I was hiding out in L.A. Michael Chamberlain had become a mystery, the somewhat pudgy young man who had disappeared, just fallen off the map, a year or so after his parents died. Every now and then, some crime show or blog would bring up my old name.

But I'd changed. My body. My name. I'd managed to keep off the grid.

Until Jason Pratt recognized my face.

"There's another story, this one out of a New Haven news site," Ira said. "How you've been sighted in Los Angeles."

Feeling hollow inside, I said, "That's not enough."

"It describes you. Says you have changed. The one thing it doesn't have is your current name."

"Pratt never found out what it is," I said.

"That doesn't mean he won't," Ira said.

"He wants money."

"You can't give it to him."

"Tell me something I don't know," I said.

"No need to be snappish," Ira said.

"I was being snarky."

"So sorry."

"Now who's snappish?" I said.

"Michael, if you—"

"If somebody wants to try to find me, there's nothing I can do about it. Until he does."

"What does that mean?" Ira said.

"I think you know," I said.

"I hope I don't," Ira said. "Maybe it's time to go back to New Haven and face the music. It was self-defense."

"I don't have any desire to do that, Ira. I just want to be left alone."

"That didn't work for Garbo," Ira said.

"She was prettier than I am," I said. "Thanks for the info."

I SPENT THE next hour putting together an investigation plan. Where to start, who to talk to, what resources I'd need. As the great philosopher Yogi Berra once said, "You've got to be careful if you don't know where you're going, 'cause you might not get there."

When twilight rolled around, it was time to eat. And by the aroma in the air the place to eat was the rally at the beach. I walked down into a crowd gathering where sand met restaurant parking lot. There was a stage on the asphalt, all decked out in red, white and blue bunting. A couple of news vans were on hand. Since it was election season in L.A. there were signs all around with the smiling face of one Allison Ursula Serret, candidate for the County Board of Supervisors. She'd be giving a speech, as would this guy Dr. Gary Pasfield, professor of integrative ecology at UCLA.

I wondered what integrative ecology meant. Maybe that a

cactus has the right to grow in the same box as a chrysanthemum.

I'm all for that.

The signs also promised a *Special Surprise Guest!*

To top it all off, free pinwheels were being passed out to the kiddies by volunteers who were only a few years removed from being kiddies themselves.

The free nachos looked about as edible as the pinwheels. So I bought an L.A. street dog from a guy with a grill trailer. L.A. street dogs are wrapped in bacon and topped with onions and one grilled *poblano* chili pepper. It's so good you don't care what your heart has to say about it. There are things worth fighting for and things worth living for, and an L.A. street dog is one of those things. The foolish rulers of Los Angeles have tried to make them illegal. But that's like trying to make the sun illegal.

If Allison Ursula Serret would come out in favor of legalizing street dogs and put that at the top of her agenda, she might just be worth voting for.

A rock band started playing onstage. They weren't bad, a foursome from that netherworld between obscurity and stardom, trying to find ways to get discovered in this age of digital downloads and YouTube virals. To break through you have be really, really good or have something really, really bad happen, like a meteor hitting the stage during a set. That would then be uploaded for the world to see and your name is made. You might be dead, but you'll be famous, and a lot of people these days seem willing to make that trade.

I wondered if my friend C Dog ever thought like that. In fact, I wondered if he ever thought at all. Or was he part of the trend, the wave of the thoughtless? Thinking takes work. You have to be taught how to do that work. But the professional educators have pretty much given up on that idea. They no longer believe that truth conquers all things, because there is no truth, only bodily fluids churning randomly around in a Darwinian jungle.

I finished the last, luscious bite of my street dog and took a walk in the throng. I was thinking there was an off chance I'd spot Brooklyn. Sometimes you just have to give the off chance an opportunity. Especially at the beginning of things.

No Brooklyn.

But plenty of beach types, curiosity seekers, political junkies wearing T-shirts with VOTE on the front, kids, and a security contingent strategically placed and looking like they all came from the same sale at Sunglass Hut.

I got back to my original vantage point as the lead singer for the rock group strangled the microphone and said, "Everybody doin' all right?"

The crowed shouted that they were.

"All riggghhhtt! Remember, we're Squealing Angst and we have some CDs for y'all. We'll be hangin' out, so come see us. But now we get to what we're here for, right?"

"Riiigghhht!"

The singer turned to his drummer and appeared to be asking what they were there for. Then he turned back to the mike and said, "All y'all are gonna love this. Y'all seen *The Formulator*, right?"

"Rigghht!"

"You know what I'm talkin' 'bout! Yeah, here he is, right here! Come on now, let's give it up for m'man Korey Halliwell!"

And there he was, bounding up onstage, one of Hollywood's royals, star of the *Formulator* movie franchise, black hair and blue eyes, former underwear model, womanizer, and recovering heroin addict. He was getting screams from the ladies and verbal high-fives from the guys.

Korey Halliwell grabbed the mike. "How y'all doin'?"

"Good!"

"Cool!"

"I love you, Korey!"

Halliwell said, "As Cliff Mack would say, we gonna do some damage!"

Everybody cheered. Cliff Mack was the name of the hero in the *Formulator* movies. *We gonna do some damage* was his catchphrase.

"We're here tonight to make some love," he said. "To make some love to the ocean, the sky, the stars, the earth, and maybe"—he paused and added with deep-throated resonance—"each other!"

More cheers, especially from the ladies.

"Earth is the only home we got, right?" Halliwell said. "So what am I lookin' at? A Skittles bag, man. Right there."

He pointed at the ground just below the stage.

"Love me some Skittles, but come on, yo! You know what that bag represents? It's guys like Harrison Delimat!"

A cacophony of boos erupted into the air. Harrison Delimat was Allison Ursula Serret's opponent in the Supervisor race.

"He's one of 'em," Korey Halliwell said. "One of the users and abusers. A raper of land, yo. And why do we let them do it? Because nobody speaks truth to power. You know what we need to do to the power?"

An actor's pause for effect.

"We gotta do some damage!"

The crowed gave up howls and cheers and maybe even a baying-at-the-moon or two.

"So I'm gonna open up my fat wallet for Allison Ursula Serret. You gotta do the same. We gotta take back the earth. Let it start here, right here in Paradise Cove. Let this be the wave that breaks across the whole country!"

Moon. Baying at.

Korey Halliwell threw a kiss to the crowd and sauntered

off the stage. He was immediately surrounded by three large men who whisked him into a waiting Town Car. Even before the next speaker got to the mike The Formulator was gone.

Then the rock band singer introduced Dr. Gary Pasfield.

A few people golf-clapped.

Pasfield was medium height, trim, bald on top with close-cropped silver hair on the side of his pate. He wore wire-rim glasses, jeans and a plaid flannel shirt.

"Hello, everyone," he said. "We all know why we're here."

Some joker shouted, "Food!"

"No, no, my friends. We are here because we can no longer be observers in the grandstand of life. When it comes to our precious Earth, we all need to get in the game. We are standing on the precipice!"

And mixing metaphors.

"We are letting others, those in power, change our world by gas emissions, imprisoning fresh water behind dams, letting the sea behind me rise with the melting of the ice caps. We no longer have a choice. We either do something or our world dies."

Some applause, some hoots, some howls, and at least one drunken epithet from a beefy and bearded man a few feet away from me. "Let's hunt some dolphins," the brute added.

Pasfield continued. "We must change things now, while we have a chance. And the one who can lead that change for us here in our beloved Southern California is a woman I once had as a student, but now count as a friend. Ladies and gentlemen, let's hear it for the next member of the Los Angeles County Board of Supervisors, Allison Ursula Serret!"

Cheers and music pumping from the stage speakers. Allison Ursula Serret walked onstage, waving. She had broad shoulders and short brown hair. She wore a baggy white sweater, black pants, and flip-flops. She knew how to dress for the beach crowd. But put her in a dark uniform and take away the politician's smile, she'd look at right at home driving a Brink's truck.

She squeezed the mike. "Thank you all so much!"

Cheers.

"Sir?"

I turned around. It was a reporter. I guessed it was a reporter because of the hand mike in her hand with the big 5 on it and a camera guy behind her. The camera guy hit me with a light.

"We'd like to interview you," she said. "If you don't mind."

"I do mind," I said.

"We won't use anything without your permission to—"

"I'm ex-Mafia," I said. "I don't want Louie the Lip to find me."

The reporter gave me a frosty stare and told her camera guy to follow. That's when I saw a woman about five feet away holding her phone up to me.

She saw me staring at her and put the phone down and gave me an I've-been-hosed look. She slipped back through the crowd. I followed and caught her by the arm.

"Let go of me!" she said. She was short and wide and had the sour look of a complaint department administrator. She was in her mid-thirties.

"I'll need to check your phone," I said.

"Get away!"

The crowd roared about something. My right hand went out of its own accord—I tell myself—and snatched the phone.

"Hey!" she said.

A few heads near me turned.

"Now Thelma," I said, "you have to take your meds!"

"Give me my phone!"

"These people are trying to listen, dear."

"That's my phone!"

I shook my head. "Do you need to go back to Dr. Alcabides?"

I thumbed her photos and found the video.

"You're stealing my phone!" she said.

"Thelma! Come along!"

I put my arm around her shoulder and pulled her toward the back edge of the crowd. She tried to wriggle out of my arm, like a bag of cats.

"Do you want the cops to take you in?" I said.

"You can't—"

I checked the vid. It was shaky and my face indistinct in the dim light. I deleted it. Even if she went to the trouble of recovering it, it wouldn't do damage. But it's the principle of the thing.

"Hey, what's up?" The beefy and bearded drunk was behind us.

"He's got my phone!" the woman said.

"She's not allowed to have a phone," I said.

"What'd she do?" Beefy said. His breath was fit for trench warfare.

"Broke out," I said.

"No!" she said.

"It's time for your meds, dear," I said.

Thelma started crying then. I powered off her phone.

And said to Beefy, "I'm going to take her to the home now."

I pulled her away from the drunk, whispering, "I'll give you back your phone once I explain things to you."

She was trembling now.

When I got her to the corner of the parking lot, I said, "I believe in the right to privacy. I don't want my likeness in somebody's phone, or on YouTube."

"I was just—" she sobbed. "You were gonna be on TV. I thought you were somebody."

"I'm barely anybody," I said. I put the phone in her hand. "I'm sorry I had to do that. Would you like to press charges?"

Her head tilted up.

"Would you like to tell a police officer I assaulted you?" I said.

"Really?"

"We can find a cop."

"I just want to go home," she said.

"Have you had dinner yet?"

"What?"

"Can I buy you a street dog?"

"Street dog?"

"You smell those onions?"

She looked around, then said, "You freak me out."

"I get that a lot," I said. I took a five from my wallet and put it in her hand. "Dinner's on me."

She didn't know whether to thank me or run screaming back to the beach. She chose a middle option, saying nothing, but giving a quick nod before turning her back.

I hung there in the corner as Allison Ursula Serret continued her speech.

"Look behind me, friends. Look at the lovely ocean, teeming with life. And then look at what people like Harrison Delimat dump into that ocean. That's the cold heart of a developer who doesn't care one bit about the environment, about the future, about the species that are dying out. These developers and technicians spew chemicals into the air and poison into our waters. They think their time is now, but we are not going to let it happen!"

That got the crowd going.

Me, too. Going back to my mobile home, that is. I've had enough of politicians. As Bierce wrote in *The Devil's Dictionary*, a politician is an eel in the fundamental mud upon which the superstructure of organized society is reared. When he wriggles he mistakes the agitation of his tail for the trembling of the edifice.

Our edifice is trembling enough as it is. The last thing we need is more politicians.

THE NEXT DAY, Wednesday, about eleven, I went to Kahuna's. A fresh-faced hostess welcomed me with a Brite-Smile. It almost blinded me. "Welcome to Kahuna's. Table for one?"

"Maybe later. I'd like to speak to one of your people. A very big guy with a Marine tat on his arm. I think his name is Kahlua."

"You mean Kalolo?"

"Ah, that's it."

The hostess laughed. "Kahlua is a drink."

"Now I recall."

She smiled and her eyes lingered. "You knew that, didn't you?"

"That Kalolo serves Kahlua at Kahuna's? Maybe."

"You're funny. He's at the bar."

THERE WAS A couple sitting at the end of the bar, near the window. The ocean was white and choppy today. There was a lone kayaker fighting his way along the caps. I envied him.

I sat at the other end of the bar and waited for the big bartender to notice me. He saw me and his face was passive. Then he recognized me and the expression changed. It was as chilly as one of the white caps outside.

He came right up to me and put his big hands on the bar top. And said nothing. His silence was as heavy as his body.

"Hi, Kalolo," I said.

"What do you want?"

"How about a Coke?"

He shook his head.

"Don't worry," I said. "I can handle it."

"You don't really want a Coke," he said.

"I'm Brooklyn's friend, remember?"

"You're not her friend."

"How do you know that?"

"She told me."

"We're on the same side here."

"I don't think so."

One of the things Joey Feint taught me was that you need to establish rapport with a recalcitrant witness. Find some common ground.

"How about those Dodgers?" I said.

Kalolo said nothing. His dark brown eyeballs gave off a simmering heat.

"I really would like that Coke," I said.

He removed his hands from the bar top and for a moment looked like he didn't know what to do with them. Then he grabbed a glass and shoveled in some ice, took the soda gun and filled the glass with Coke. He put a little napkin down and placed the glass on top of it.

"Do you have a slice of lemon?" I asked.

He shook his head.

There were lemon slices and cherries within reach.

I looked at them.

Kalolo looked at them.

I smiled.

Kalolo didn't smile.

"I was hoping you might help me find her," I said. "She's missing."

Kalolo didn't smile even more.

"Last time I saw her was here," I said. "With you. When's the last time you saw her?"

The bartender said, "Finish and go. It's on the house."

Ironic, coming from a guy who was the size of a house.

I reached over for a handful of lemons. He would have to do some more slicing now. I squeezed the citrus into the Coke. Some of the juice splashed on the bar top. I put the rinds down in a pile and took a sip of the Coke.

I squinted. "Sour," I said. "And let that be a lesson to you."

I got up and left.

THERE'S A SMALL sliver of beach access behind Kahuna's. You have to hop a chain-link fence and climb over some rocks. And ignore the *No Trespassing* signs the Colony crowd put up.

I'm good at ignoring signs.

I went down to the beach, took off my flip-flops, and started walking, looking at the houses. Back in the day when they were first built, people called them shacks. These shacks now fetched three million or more. And I was sure that out of one of these Brooklyn Christie had stumbled with poison pumping into her bloodstream.

Joey Feint always talked about "shoe leather" being the key to a good investigation. He meant you walk a lot of streets, knock on a lot of doors, talk to a lot of people.

My only shoe leather was bare feet on very exclusive sand, but I was sure there was someone in one of these places I needed to talk to.

The beach was virtually empty, consistent with the exclusivity theme. A man with a tan and Speedos and a phone stood at water's edge. He was gesturing with one hand as he spoke into the phone. He looked at me as I walked by. He seemed surprised there was somebody else on the beach.

He went back to gesturing.

Up ahead I saw another denizen. A woman sitting in a beach chair positioned about halfway between the water and one of the homes.

She had blonde hair done up retro-style. The Jean Harlow look was making a comeback. What's old eventually becomes new in Hollywood and Malibu. I wondered when the Laurel & Hardy look would come around again and I'd see men walking the beach in derbies, fiddling with their ties.

This Harlow had on big, round sunglasses and wore a sheer, black beach dress over her bikini. Her legs were long and smooth and crossed at the ankles. She was reading a hardcover book.

"Excuse me," I said.

She looked up. Paused. Then pushed her sunglasses up to her platinum-blonde hair.

Her face seemed sculpted out of porcelain, for nature does not work with such precision. The normal human face has nuances and nerves and a certain elasticity. The face that looked at me did not seem capable of wrinkling. Or smiling. Or making any sudden moves.

"This is a private beach," she said.

"Is it?" I said.

"How did you get here?"

"I live in Paradise Cove."

She closed the hardcover. Then she gave me a lingering gaze, like a horse breeder assessing stock.

It was hard to guess her age, but I figured somewhere north of forty.

"You look like someone who belongs on a beach," she said. "Just not this one."

"I believe the sand is not owned by anyone," I said.

"We get the occasional troublemaker," she said. "Why don't you just move along?"

"What are you reading?"

She held up the book. It was a James Patterson.

"Is it good?" I asked.

"It doesn't have to be," she said.

While I was trying to figure out what she meant, she stood and tossed the book on the beach chair. She folded the chair and put it under her arm, started walking away.

"Can I ask you something first?" I said.

She stopped and turned. "Who are you?"

"I'm looking for a woman—"

"Oh?"

"—who may have been hanging around the beach over this way."

"Is she your woman?"

"No."

"Then why are you looking for her?"

"She's been reported missing."

The woman's blue-velvet eyes turned inquisitive. "Are you some kind of detective?"

"I am looking into the matter on behalf of a family member. This woman had long, dark hair, worn straight. Mid-twenties. Tall and ..."

"And?"

"Well, I mean ..."

"Nice body?"

"Not that I go out of my way to notice," I said.

"Listen, sweets," she said with a slight curl of her lip. "We want you to notice."

My interview was not going the direction I had anticipated.

"You know," she said, "I can't really think in the morning without a Bloody Mary. Have one?"

"I don't think so, but—"

"I really think you should," she said.

"Why is that?"

"Because I believe I know the woman you mean."

I FOLLOWED HER up some wooden steps to a redwood

deck that held a four-chair patio set and one immaculate stainless steel barbecue grill. We went inside through a sliding glass door. She opened it first.

The inside was hardwood floor, rugs, soft furniture, and pillows. There was a bar in the corner of the expansive living room.

"Let me fix us the drinks," the woman said as she stepped behind the bar.

"Nothing for me."

"Oh, come on. Join me."

"This really isn't a social call," I said.

She trained her blue-velvet eyes on me. "My name is Nikki. What's yours?"

"Mike."

"We are now social. Have one with me."

"Can we talk about the woman first?"

"No."

She opened what I presumed was a small refrigerator. She brought up a can of V-8 tomato juice and placed it on the bar top. Did the same with a bottle of Stolichnaya vodka, followed in order by Tabasco, and Lea & Perrins Worcestershire sauce. Then she placed a silver cocktail shaker and two highball glasses with gilt rivulets next to the ingredients.

"How long have you lived at the Cove?" she said as she opened the Stoli.

"Not long," I said.

"Where you from?"

"Here and there."

"Nicely mysterious," she said.

She poured a healthy amount of vodka into the shaker. Put in a little less of the V-8, which, according to Hoyle, should be the more copious of the two. She expertly dashed in the Tabasco and Worcestershire and followed that up with some salt and pepper.

"Nikki, I don't want to take up more time than—"

"Yes you do," she said. "Or you don't know your own mind."

She grabbed some ice cubes from the below—"Pardon my fingers, sweets"—and tossed them in the shaker. She put the shaker top on and began the maraca routine. As she shook it, she looked at me coolly. She hadn't smiled once.

Nikki poured the Marys into the glasses and went to the fridge once more, coming up with a couple of lemon slices and two stalks of celery. She put one lemon slice on the rim of each glass and dunked the celery stalks.

You cannot say she was not prepared.

She walked the drinks over and handed me one.

Not wanting to insult her, I accepted it.

"I like things spicy," she said. "Tell me what you think."

"You mean about the drink?"

"You are sweet. Let's sit over here." She placed herself on a plush sofa and patted the spot next to her. I took a spot a little further away.

"So you said you knew the woman I'm looking for," I said.

"How's your drink?" Nikki said.

"Fine."

"You haven't tried it."

"I saw you make it."

She put her lips on her glass. Kept them there a moment. Then she took a sip.

"Any information you have would be appreciated,' I said.

"I may have seen her. When did she disappear?"

"Sometime over the last few days. When did you see her?"

"I said I *may* have seen her. I'm not exactly the sheriff of the beach."

"You just want people kicked off it."

"You're not exactly friendly, are you?" she said.

"I'm not here as a friend," I said.

"We can change that."

She put her drink on the glass-top coffee table and coiled her legs up onto the sofa.

"I want you to know, Mike, I never do this. Strange men from the beach. But there's something about you I really like."

It had been only ten minutes from beach to this.

"You shouldn't be doing this," I said.

"Why not?"

"I could be dangerous."

"Are you?"

"A psychopath."

"You don't sound like a psychopath."

"That could be one of my tricks," I said.

"Is it a trick?"

I put my drink on the table. "Can you answer my question? Then I should move along."

"Don't hurry," Nikki said. "I'll behave myself, if you really want me to."

"I think that would be best."

A door slammed. I almost dropped my Bloody Mary.

"Great," she said.

"What?"

"My husband's home."

HE WAS A good-looking sixty or so. Full head of gray hair. In shape, and wore a blue suit and perfectly knotted tie.

"Another one?" he said dryly.

"Your mind is in the gutter, as usual," Nikki said.

"Where I found you," he said.

"Sir, if I can explain," I said.

"No need," he said. "I know the whole thing. I suppose I should kill you now. Kill you both, in fact."

"Don't be dull," Nikki said.

"I'd get off light," he said. "And it would be worth it."

"Where are we having dinner tonight, dear?" Nikki said.

The man took off his coat and tossed it on a stool near the wet bar. He took some keys out of his pocket and unlocked something behind the bar.

I just stood there like a dolt.

The man came up with a healthy looking revolver and pointed it at me.

"Why don't you go out to the beach, honey?" the man said. "I want to talk to your stud."

I said, "I refuse to be shot under false pretenses."

"Watch yourself," Nikki said to me as she swept on by. She went out the sliding door and closed it behind her.

"Nice marriage you've got," I said.

The man nodded. He sighed. "You said you wanted to explain."

"Put the gun down, huh?"

"Tell me what's going on," he said.

So I explained to him about Brooklyn, about scoping out the beach, about finding his wife reading a book. About how she lured me into this den of iniquity.

When I finished the man looked resigned to the hand fate had dealt him. "I believe you," he said, lowering the gun. "That's Nikki all over. You can go now."

"I appreciate that," I said. "No hard feelings. But I'd like to ask if you might have spotted this woman, Brooklyn, maybe out there on the beach or walking around."

He shook his head. "But if you want to know which of these homes she came out of, you can start three houses that way." He pointed with the gun toward the Cove. "Remember Jon-Scott Morrow?"

"Sure," I said. Morrow had shot to movie stardom in the late eighties in a tragic love story about a young man and an older woman played by Ann-Margret. He was *People* magazine's Sexiest Man of the Year around 1990 or so. But his star faded when critics woke up to the fact that his acting range started at A and ground to a halt at B. I hadn't heard much about him, except that his teenage son died of a heroin overdose about ten years ago.

"Then why don't you take your investigation out that way?" he said. "You don't have to speak to my wife again."

"I wouldn't have done it anyway."

"Man, I wish I was you." He put the gun on the bar and started to make himself a drink.

I let myself out.

Nikki was sitting in the same chair, lost in her thriller. I walked along the sand to the third house from hers.

Where I saw a big guy in a black T-shirt and black jeans and bare feet. He was standing on the deck, his elbows resting on the wooden railing as he looked at the beach through binoculars.

I fished out Ira's lawyer card from my wallet and held it up. "Greetings," I said. "Mind if I ask a question or two?"

The big guy lowered the binoculars. He was about my age, with roid-pumped muscles. Jacked up for intimidation, not functionality. I was not impressed.

"About what?" he said.

"A missing girl. Around twenty-five or six. Black hair. Tall and beautiful."

"Which is like every chick around here."

"Here?"

He gestured toward the beach.

"Is Mr. Morrow at home?" I said.

Big Guy stiffened. "Where'd you get that information?"

"It's not a secret, is it?"

"Mr. Morrow likes his privacy. Like everybody else on this strip."

"I keep getting that impression," I said. "Maybe you could go in and see if he'd talk to me."

"I don't have to ask."

"Ask anyway."

Big Guy swung his legs over the rail. Then he jumped off and landed on the sand in front of me. He puffed out his chest. I almost laughed.

"Drift," he said.

"How many times do I have to explain that this is a public beach?"

"Not as long as I'm around."

"Meaning?"

"You don't want to find out," he said.

"You wouldn't last two rounds. Your arms couldn't stay up. Your pecs are cosmetic, not supportive. And your range of motion has got to be a thing of horror."

"You want to try me?"

"It's too nice a day and we're in Malibu, where the living is easy. I'm just trying to do a job. I'm not going to be a problem. I'll ask—"

"What's going on, Claude?"

I looked up at the deck. It was Jon-Scott Morrow. His face was the same, though puffier and with more lines than when Ann-Margret seduced him in *Love in Season*.

No doubt he'd bought into Malibu when he was hot. Now that he was not, he at least was sitting on a sand dune of equity.

He wore a light-blue terrycloth robe that was cinched against a paunch and ended above knobby, pallid knees. His curly hair, which had once been a wheat-colored thatch that drove women wild, was now in major recession and mostly gray.

Claude said, "I got this, Mr. Morrow."

"What, exactly, have you got?" Morrow said.

"I was just about to get him to leave," Claude said.

"Mr. Morrow," I said, "I'm on official business and if I could ask just a couple of questions, I'll be on my way."

"You're not police, are you?" Morrow asked.

"No. I'm working for a private party."

"Then I don't have to answer anything, do I?"

"You don't," I said. "But it would be a great favor to me if you would."

"Clear him away," Morrow said to Claude.

"Let's go," Claude said, and then made his first mistake. He put his hand on my shoulder.

I GAVE CLAUDE an old-fashioned cup-slap to both ears. Bam. Pounding the ears like that causes disequilibrium and sometimes a concussion. I didn't go all out because I kind of felt sorry for what I was about to do to Claude in front of his employer.

Next it was a matter of putting my right thumb between the thumb and forefinger of Claude's left hand. Then, with my left hand I grabbed his left elbow and turned my body so we were both facing the same way. At the same time I pulled his elbow up. With simple pressure applied to his hand and wrist I now controlled him completely.

"Where would you like me to put him?" I said to Morrow.

"You let him go!" Morrow said.

"Why?"

"I'll call the police!"

"Please do," I said.

Claude tried to move away from me. I upped the pressure on his hand.

Claude yelped.

"All right," Morrow said. "Just let him go and I'll talk to you."

"Did you hear that Claude?" I asked.

Claude nodded.

"Don't try anything stupid," I said.

I let him go to his visible relief. He started rubbing his left hand. His eyes were watery. He looked at me and said, "You're a dead man."

Then he made his second mistake.

He poked my chest with a steroidal index finger.

Which hurts.

And pain annoys me.

So I gave Claude a side kick to his ribs. It was lightning fast and I was rather pleased with myself.

As he *oomphed* I moved behind and roped him with a Mata Leão. That's a choke hold that can easily become lethal. I now controlled the amount of oxygen going to Claude's brain.

"I don't like your professional manner, Claude," I said. "You're like a Visigoth strutting around Rome."

Claude said nothing. Maybe it was because he didn't understand my reference. More likely it was because I was choking him and he was about eight seconds from unconsciousness.

I let up on him a little. He sucked in a pitiful gasp.

I said, "I'm going to let you go now. I want you to sit here on the sand with your right leg over your left. If you uncross your legs I'll kick your head and put you in this hold again. Is that clear, Claude?"

I took off the choke hold but put both hands around his throat. At the same time, I pushed the crook of his knee with my heel and guided him down to a sitting position.

"Now stick your legs out and cross them," I said.

He tried to get up. He made it about an inch before I cut off his air supply.

"Just do it, Claude," Jon-Scott Morrow said.

Claude dropped back on the sand. Then crossed his legs. I let him breathe again.

Morrow said, "You've gone to an awful lot of trouble just to ask me a question."

"And I'm a little cranky, too."

"What's this about?"

"I'm looking into the disappearance of a woman named Brooklyn Christie. Does that name mean anything to you?"

"Who told you to talk to me?"

"I keep my sources confidential," I said. "But that applies to you, too. Anything you tell me stays between us."

"What did you say her name was?"

"Brooklyn Christie."

"What does she look like?"

"She looks like a model. Tall. Long, dark hair."

Claude uncrossed his legs.

I slapped the back of his head.

He crossed them again.

Morrow said, "I know a great many models."

"Did you have a party here a week ago?"

"I don't see as I have to answer any more questions."

"I can be a regular nuisance," I said.

"So can the police, who I'm going to call now."

"Let it go, Jon," I said. "We'll have another chat sometime."

"I don't think so," Morrow said. "Next time Claude will be more prepared."

"That right, Claude?" I said.

"Wait and see," Claude said.

"Check your underwear for sand fleas," I said.

NOT MUCH HAPPENED on my walk back to the Cove.

Unless you count the explosion.

It was distant but distinct. Not the kind of thing you hear on a nice, sunny day in L.A. You're more likely to hear gunfire than a bomb or dynamite. It was loud enough to get most of the beach goers looking over their shoulders. It came from the Topanga Canyon direction, south. But that was all I could tell.

I registered the sound in my brain, filing it under TBLAL—to be looked at later. Then I went to my crib to jot down some notes in a chronology I would turn in later to Ray Christie.

There wasn't much to report, of course, but one of the things Joey Feint taught me was that clients, more than anything else, just want to know that you're working for them. Doing something. And keeping in touch about it.

That's the basis of world religions, too. Everybody would like to know that a deity is doing something for them and keeping in touch about it.

Those who give up on that hope are called atheists.

Those who hope they might be able to hope again are called agnostics.

Those who never give any thoughts to these matters are called fools.

Those who keep going over and over things because the psyche shifts around are called wanderers in the earth.

My category.

As I was typing away on the laptop Ira had generously donated to me, I heard a knock on my screen door.

C Dog. And he looked like he'd been crying.

I waved him in.

"Oh, man!" he said, closing the screen behind him.

"What's wrong?"

"My ax, man! My Paul Reed Smith! That guy ripped it off me!"

"What guy?"

"That guy from the beach, you shoved seaweed in his mouth."

"When did this happen?"

"Just now!"

He wailed like sad dog, put his face in his hands.

"Sit down," I said. "Take a deep breath."

"I want you to get him," he said. "I want you to find him and rip his lungs out."

"I'm not a hit man, C. Let's go to the police with this."

"I can't, man."

"Why not?"

He sighed. "Outstanding warrant."

"Sit down, C."

He plopped himself on the futon. "What is wrong with this world?"

"Much," I said.

C DOG SAID, "What am I gonna do?"

"Tell me what happened," I said.

He waved toward the ocean. "I'm just sitting out there, minding my own business, practicing unplugged, you know?"

"Were you high?"

"What's that got to do with anything?"

I glared at him.

"Yes," he said.

"Go on," I said.

"So he comes up to me and says, 'Cool guitar.' He knows I know who he is. He says, I really want a guitar like that, can I have it? And I try to laugh but he pushes me down and takes it, just rips it off. Then he hit me in the back of the freaking head and I'm like lying there wondering what just happened and what is wrong with this freaking world!"

"The world would be a great place if not for the people," I said.

"You got that right! And there was nothin' I could do, he's too big! Why would he do that?"

"To bait me," I said.

"What's that mean?"

"I know the type," I said. "I shamed him. Instead of coming at me directly, he came after somebody weaker."

"Hey!"

"You don't have to remain that way," I said.

"I just want my guitar back, man. Can you help me?"

"I might."

"Might?"

"You'll have to pay me," I said.

"Oh, man, I can't pay you. I don't have spare money."

"You have enough to buy pot," I said.

He threw up his hands.

I said, "Tell you what. I'll do it for no money. But we will enter into an agreement."

"What do you mean?" he said.

"You agree to do some things for me."

"Like what?"

"First thing is, you stop firing up."

"What!"

"You're going to get off weed."

"Oh come on!"

"That's condition number one."

C Dog stood up and circled around, just like a real dog looking for a place to lie down and, not finding one, growled.

"That's outrageous, man!" he said.

"Is it?" I said.

"You expect me to give up smoking a little?"

"You smoke a lot."

"Yeah! So?"

"You want your guitar back?"

His mouth dropped open like a drawbridge at some medieval castle.

"You don't have to turn this into Sophie's choice," I said.

"Who's that?"

"A character in a famous novel. She had to decide which one of her children to give up to the Nazis to be killed."

"Whack."

"This is only a guitar and some weed," I said. "So what will it be?"

"You're killin' me."

"I will also teach you how to defend yourself."

He perked up. "Really?"

"You want to learn?"

He nodded.

"Then you must also learn virtue."

C Dog plopped back down on the futon, defeated. But in that defeat I could see the beginnings of his reconstruction.

"Man, who *are* you?" C Dog said. "You're not like any dude I ever met before."

"You will become unique as well, C Dog. We cannot master anything until we master ourselves."

"Can I …"

"Can you what?"

"Have one more bowl? For the road?"

"That road is now closed, C Dog. Yes or no?"

"Oh, man!"

"You can have a Coke. They're in the refrigerator."

C Dog got up, shook his head like he'd been dinged. Which he had. Then he shuffled toward the refrigerator, looking like a soul in purgatory.

I CALLED IRA.

"Any luck with Brooklyn Christie?" I said.

"Training and skill," Ira said. "Luck has nothing to do with it."

"I'll concede the point."

"As well you should."

"Don't force me to construct an argument, Ira."

"I would cut you to ribbons."

"Uncle," I said.

"Good," Ira said. "I found a last known address for Brooklyn Christie. But it's not by the beach. It's out in Sherman Oaks. An apartment. You ought to swing by."

"I'll do that now," I said. "Hey, I heard an explosion, about an hour ago. Can you try to find out what it was?"

"Tell me more," he said.

"It sounded like major demolition, something like that. Not far from the Cove."

I heard him clacking the keyboard. There is comfort in Ira's typing. He was one of the first computer ops in Mossad. A bullet put him in a wheelchair. But his head and hands were as awesome as ever.

After a minute or so, Ira said, "There does appear to be something here. CHP is closing PCH from Sunset to Topanga. That's going to be one royal mess at rush hour."

"Where'd it happen?" I said.

"They don't say exactly. But I'm looking at a satellite feed that refreshes every twenty minutes or so. There's something of a disturbance in the hills right above the Getty Villa."

That would be J. Paul Getty's former home. The outrageously wealthy oil man had fashioned the place like a Roman emperor's summer retreat. It housed an invaluable collection of Greek and Roman art and stuck its nose over PCH, pointed at the ocean.

"Think that's it?" I said.

"Don't know yet. I'm fast, but not a miracle worker."

"Guess what?" I said.

"They found Amelia Earhart."

"Close. I have a date."

"A date date?" Ira said.

"A first date."

"As if you were in high school?"

"I skipped high school."

"Be kind and considerate," Ira said.

"I was thinking of being charming," I said.

"Don't pull a muscle," Ira said.

SHERMAN OAKS IS a prosperous slice of the San Fernando Valley. It backs up into the hills that look down on Ventura Boulevard and a thriving commercial and shopping district. Here is old L.A. money invested in what was once a bucolic retreat from the hubbub of Hollywood and downtown.

Brooklyn's lowland building was a two-story on Magnolia. It was situated to the right of a McMansion, one of those over-built homes on a simple, middle-class street. The McMansion looked like an ostentatious woman's hat, complete with ostrich feathers. Only instead of feathers it was palm trees and white birch.

On the other side of Brooklyn's place was a similar apartment building, with a wide driveway separating the two complexes.

Brooklyn's unit was number 2, in the front corner.

I knocked on the door, waited. No answer.

I went to the next unit down, number 4. Knocked. Waited. Knocked again.

Nothing.

Then a scraping sound. Only it wasn't coming from the apartment. It was at the back edge of the building.

A mirror, deep set inside a blue plastic housing, jutted from the edge of the building. In the mirror I thought I could make out a small pair of eyes.

A kid's periscope.

I was being watched.

"You got me," I said.

The periscope pulled back.

I waited.

Slowly it came back.

I waved.

It disappeared.

I knocked on the door again. Still nothing.

"Sure wish I knew who lived here," I said.

The periscope came out about an inch.

"Yes indeed, I sure wish somebody could tell me who lives here."

The periscope stayed put. Then I heard a small voice say, "Desiree."

A boy's voice.

"Desiree lives here?" I said.

The mystery voice said, "Uh-huh."

"I wish I knew where she was."

"Store," the voice said.

"You must be the watcher of the building, huh?"

"Uh-huh."

"My name's Mike."

"Uh-huh."

"Do you know Brooklyn?"

"Uh-huh."

"Have you seen Brooklyn lately?"

"Uh-uh."

"Why don't you come out and talk?"

The bit of periscope receded.

I waited for the watcher to appear.

He did not.

I went to the back of the building. There was a carport there with four spaces.

But no boy with a periscope. Well, this was his territory. He had to know all the best hiding places.

I was about to venture to the other side of the building and check with another neighbor when a red Hyundai pulled into one of the carport spaces.

A woman about forty got out and gave me a quick eye, then popped her trunk and pulled out a blue bag with straps. The bag said *Trader Joe's* on the side.

She started walking toward unit number four.

"Desiree?" I said.

She almost jumped out of her blue jeans. She had shoulder-length auburn hair and a Roman nose. She looked at me like I was a Carthaginian.

"I'm a friend of Brooklyn's," I said.

She held up her keys. "Don't come near me."

I saw her thumb on something. A little pepper spray canister.

"Her father hired me," I said.

"Then you're not her friend," she said.

"Can I explain?"

"Stay there."

"She's missing."

Desiree paused. "What do you mean?"

"Her father wants to find her and I'm trying to help. Can we talk a minute?"

"You can't come inside."

"Out here will work." We were standing in the middle of the asphalt lot.

Out of the corner of my eye I saw something move. It was my little periscope friend again, this time on the opposite side of the building.

"Go on the other side of my car," Desiree said.

"Sure."

I went under the carport cover on the far side of her Hyundai. She got under the shade, keeping the car between us. She also kept her thumb on the pepper spray.

I took a well-worn *Ira Rosen, Attorney-at-Law* card out of my wallet. I placed it on the roof of the car.

"I work for a lawyer. I'm an investigator."

She took the card, looked it over.

"I have to put my groceries away," she said.

"I won't take long."

Desiree looked around, as if to see if anyone was listening. Or around to look at me.

"All right," she said. "You can come in. But I'm leaving the door open. There's lots of people in this building."

"I like a close-knit community," I said.

THERE ARE APARTMENTS that feel transitory, like the person inside wants to get out and buy something as soon as possible. Or get married. Or move in with a boyfriend. Or go back to the parents' home in Toledo.

Then there are places that feel permanent, well lived-in, last stop—unless you hit the lottery.

Desiree's apartment had a last-stop feel to it.

Her furniture showed its years, though nothing was messy or about to fall apart. There was a *People* magazine on a coffee table next to an official California voter guide addressed to Desiree Parks at this address.

A fat gray cat jumped onto a chair and checked me out the way felines do—assessing if I was worth the time of day or a doofus to be ignored.

"That's Silverado," Desiree said. "He's friendly."

"Won't he try to get out?"

"No. Total house cat."

Desiree set her bag of groceries on the kitchen counter. She opened the refrigerator and started putting items away.

"You can sit down," she said.

I sat on the sofa. Silverado stared at me.

Desiree came back to the living room. She still held her keys, though her thumb was off the pepper spray.

"Okay," she said.

I said, "I helped Brooklyn the other day. I live at the beach, Paradise Cove, and she was there one morning when I was running. She was sick. I got her some help. She was grateful, we had a meal together, breakfast. A few days later her father comes to me and says she's missing. I want to help him find her. She was living in number two, right?"

Desiree nodded. "I don't know her all that well. She pretty much is out all the time. I guess when you look like she does, you're not going to be spending a lot of time alone."

"There are different ways to be alone," I said.

She nodded, like she knew exactly what that meant.

"There was one time," she said, "when Brooklyn came over here. She was a little drunk. She was depressed about something and she wanted to talk to me. People always want to talk to me, I don't know what it is."

"It's not a bad quality to have," I said.

"Always the friend, never the … whatever. So she was saying how she got her shot, which I think meant her shot at becoming a star."

"She said she got it?"

"Got it and it didn't work out was the impression I got. She said she was supposed to be in a movie with this big star, but she wouldn't say who. She only said they're all … she used a word I don't like to say."

"I can guess," I said.

She got quiet then, and looked at her hands.

"Is there something else?" I said.

She pursed her lips, then said, "Something kind of crazy."

"What is it?"

Desiree said, "She started talking about somebody named Michael. Went on and on about Michael was coming. Finally I asked her who this guy was, and she said he wasn't a guy, he was an angel. In fact, he was some kind of other angel ... a ..."

"Archangel?"

"That's it. What is that?"

"In the Bible, the archangel Michael is depicted as the leader of the heavenly army, and he does battle against Satan. In the Book of Revelation, Satan is a dragon and Michael and his angels go to war against him."

"Really?"

"That's the story, anyway."

"She said Michael was really coming, to save the earth. And she knew where he was going to show up and was going to see him."

"Did she say where this was going to happen?"

Desiree shook her head.

"Can you think of anything else she might have said, any kind of name or place?"

"I'm sorry, I really can't ... wait, no, there was a friend. She said she had a friend and they were going off together someplace, someday."

"Can you recall the name of this friend?"

"Linda ... no, Lindsay. That was it."

"Lindsay who?"

"She didn't give a last name."

"Okay. Thanks. You've been a help."

"I hope so. I hope you find her."

I nodded.

"Pretty weird to believe in angels, huh?"

"I don't know," I said, standing. "There are weirder things people believe."

"Like what?" she said.

"Oh, that you can make nice with evil and it'll make nice with you."

She blinked.

I nodded and left.

BUT WHAT DID I believe?

Who was I to say there wasn't any archangel Michael? Maybe he was out there right now, planning a comeback, and maybe Brooklyn was one of those crazy people who turns out not to be crazy after all, but has an insight that everybody else misses and ignores.

Traffic was hellish all the way to Las Virgenes, so I had some thoughts about eternal damnation. It would be one big traffic jam, everybody honking at each other and cursing and sometimes whipping out a gun and blasting. And you'd move about ten feet every million years and then, boom, you'd be right back at the beginning again.

When I got to the Cove the sun was sticking its feet in the ocean. I went to the sand and watched until night flowed over Los Angeles. And the thought came to me, distant and blinking like a star, but definite—Brooklyn Christie was probably dead.

NEXT MORNING I went to Ira's to fill him in on my meeting with Desiree.

"You are really playing the role now, aren't you?" Ira said.

"I'm making honest money doing work for our client."

"He is not our client yet. I haven't even met the man."

"Trust me," I said. "He's our client."

"Your use of the word *our* is troubling," Ira said.

"Now isn't it time you did a little work?" I said.

Eyebrows narrowing, Ira gave me something of a low growl.

I said, "Put your thinking yarmulke on. Desiree mentioned that Brooklyn started talking about the archangel Michael, and how he was coming back."

"Archangel Michael?"

"He figures in Revelation, right?"

"Yes, but if you'll recall, Mr. Romeo, I am a Jew. What I know of Michael is from the prophet Daniel and the post-canonical period."

"The name means the one who is like God, right?" I said.

Ira shook his head. "No, in the Hebrew the name is a rhetorical question, 'Who is like God?' Meaning, no one."

"I'll buy that."

"I'm not selling. It's just the truth. You take it or leave it."

"I'll wait."

With a sigh, Ira said, "The prophet Daniel's final vision is concerned with the course of eastern Mediterranean political history, from the fall of the Persian Empire through the reign of the Seleucid emperor Antiochus IV Epiphanes."

"Somehow I don't think that is of interest to Brooklyn Christie."

Ira gave me a long look. "You're thinking something."

"Just a thought," I said.

"I already established that. A thought about *what?*"

"I have this feeling she's dead."

"Why would you think that?" Ira said.

"No explanation."

"Then it's irrational, isn't it?"

"Is it?" I said. "Don't you believe in intuition?"

"I believe in evidence," Ira said. "And connections."

"So why don't you give the computer a little spin and see

what you can find out? Do I have to do all the heavy lifting around here?"

"There's a turkey leg in my freezer," Ira said. "Bring it to me so I can beat you with it."

I did not get it. I went out to the back yard where I'd spent some good days trying to get my life back into a consistent and helpful motion again. There was a bench and some chairs here and a nice shade tree. I sat under the tree and thought about Desiree. There had been something in her voice that I couldn't quite identify when I was there.

It wasn't fear, though that could have been the undercurrent. It was more like she expected a shoe to drop. What kind of shoe? A light pump or a steel-toed boot? And why?

Maybe she was just nervous around me. Maybe she never quite let her guard down. Which I could understand. I'm not usually one to set people at ease.

But there was something dangling out there that wasn't a dead end. Joey Feint said you found that in every case. There was always something that bothered you, like the missing piece of a jigsaw puzzle. But you couldn't force it. The piece had a specific shape and all you could do was find it.

If you didn't, you'd never forget about it. It would be one of those cases that gnawed at you. Get enough of them and booze could become your palliative, as it had for Joey.

After a few more minutes of chasing my mental tail I went back in the house. Where I heard Ira murmuring, "Well, well, well."

"What'd you find?" I said.

"A curious confluence of events. I like it when that happens."

Ira wheeled himself back a bit so he could face me. "That explosion you heard, it was at a development site in the hills just above where the Getty is. That's all supposed to be protected space, until recently."

"What happened?"

"There was a push-through exception made. There's supposed to be a tract of high-end homes. There was equipment up there, big cats and heavy machinery to start scraping. Most of that was blown up. So was a general contractor named Sykes."

"So now it's murder."

"And the murderer wants us to know who he is. This was posted on a website not half an hour ago. It was obtained anonymously, but the author is claiming responsibility for the explosion. Sit down and read it."

I pulled a chair over the computer and looked at the screen.

Let these 10 theses be a warning and a call to awaken to the Spirit of the World

1. Mankind has machined itself into oblivion, wreaking havoc upon the Earth. Those countries that purport to lead the world vis-a-vis economic "progress" have visited poison, death, destruction and destitution upon the Fourth World. Nature herself is being destroyed. Nature herself, under her own laws, is entitled to self-defense. The aggressor shall be stopped.

2. Systems are inherently evil.

3. It is permissible to use violence against evil.

4. If evil is allowed to continue without opposition, it will inevitably deaden the spirit of the world. The spirit of the world is not material, by virtue of the very definition of the word. The spirit of the world has always existed and always will exist. It was not created. It is itself the creative force. It has no one personality. It is everything and everywhere.

5. Rapists of the land are in bondage to the system, and therefore are slaves who unwittingly advance evil. We hold no animosity toward slaves. But slaves must be freed, either by removing them from the system or taking their lives—for in death there is also freedom, if one is enslaved to evil.

6. Children are indoctrinated into the system almost from birth. There are some exceptions to this, but not many. The entire edifice must be brought down to save the many. If the few are sacrificed in the effort, that is not "collateral damage." It is in fact dying for the greatest cause of all—the salvation of the Earth.

7. There is One who oversees the Earth and leads armies to protect it. Anyone who is seeking to despoil the Earth is at war against it, and thus is rightly opposed by the Army of Light.

8. The One who oversees the Earth is named Michael, and he is among us.

9. There is no legitimate Jewish state.

10. There is only one option for mankind on Earth, and that is to surrender to Michael and cease war. A refusal to do this will only result in more warfare and bloodshed. All building must stop. A return to the Earth and simplicity, or death.

"NOW, GRASSHOPPER," IRA said when I'd finished, "what strikes you as odd about this document?"

"You mean besides the whole thing?" I said.

"Think, boy, that's what you're supposed to be good at."

I scanned the theses again. "Number nine is out of place."

"Why is that?" Ira said.

"Wasn't the angel Michael a protector of Israel?"

"By Jove, you've done it!"

"Don't sound so surprised," I said.

"Now, what's the connection?" Ira said.

"From Brooklyn to Michael to an explosion to this document. Related?"

"Maybe and maybe not," Ira said.

"I'm so glad we had this chat," I said.

"What else might this be?" Ira said.

He looked at me with his Socratic gaze. He loves doing this. So I furrowed my brow to make him believe I was thinking.

Which I was.

Finally, I said, "It's a signature."

Ira smiled, nodded. "Like something one of those movie serial killers leaves behind, so the cop can eventually catch him."

"This guy's an anti-Semite who just can't help himself?"

"I like that theory," Ira said. "Let me keep that in mind as I do more digging."

"You keep digging," I said. "I have another matter to attend to."

"Ah, your date."

"Yes."

"I shall pray for her."

JOHN "THUNDER" MCMAHON was the toughest man I ever fought.

He looked like the devil's pit bull and smelled like no other human I've ever been nose-close to. His was a scent somewhere between a garbage scow and Mississippi road kill. He was from Jackson, actually, and I do believe he worked on his smell as much as on his grappling.

It was one of his advantages.

The other was extremely long arms at the end of which were massive paws. He was a freak of nature or, as Seinfeld once noted about "Man Hands," something out of Greek mythology.

And mean.

And a cheater.

It took every skill I knew, and the ability to hold my breath, to get him to tap out.

This was who I thought of when I was around Sophie. It was a trick my mind played on me. It was telling me I was better off in a cage than in an intimate setting with a woman.

Especially one who could knock me out with a look.

She smiled from a booth when I walked into Hammett's at noon. She had a book on the table along with a coffee cup.

I had my best shirt on, a Hawaiian number I'd nabbed at a Tommy Bahama outlet store. I was shaved and presentable, at least in my own estimation.

"Any trouble finding the place?" she said.

"Not at all," I said. The trouble was in my nervous stomach.

I was not a popular kid in school. I was always the youngest in class because they'd move me up, and up. I was a chunk, too. Consequently, the girls looked past me. Or around me. I did not do the dating thing. I never learned how.

So here I was trying to figure it out on the fly, suddenly in the grip of something even stronger than Thunder McMahon's mighty meat hooks.

"What are you reading?" I said quickly, heading to the safety of our common ground.

"Joan Didion," she said. "*Slouching Toward Bethlehem.* I'm researching the 1960s, trying to figure out what happened."

"My parents came out of the sixties and made it to maturity."

"What do your parents do?"

"They taught. They're no longer alive."

The change in subject got rid of my nerves and replaced them with the sadness that is always there when I think of them.

Sophie's face was warm, comforting.

"I bet they were good at what they did," she said.

"Why would you bet that?" I said, a little too snappishly.

"Only from my conversations with you, brief as they've been."

I should have apologized to her.

Instead, I nodded my head.

A waitress came over and handed us menus and told us the special was a cottage cheese and potato hand roll with cashews and tamarind sauce.

I ordered coffee.

"I want to teach," Sophie said. "High school."

"Why high school?"

"I had an English teacher in high school who practically saved my life. I guess I'd like to be able to do that, too."

There was a lot underneath that but I decided it was too early to ask.

"The first time I saw you," I said, "you had a UCLA sweatshirt on."

"I'm working on my Masters," she said. "American lit."

I nodded. I was getting good at nodding.

"What kind of work do you do, Mike?"

There it was. How much could I tell her? No, how little could I tell her without seeming like I was hiding something? I should have rehearsed something. You don't avoid moments by wishing them away.

I SAID, "I used to be in the entertainment business, but I'm working for a lawyer at the moment."

"What part of the entertainment business? My grandfather worked at MGM."

"I never got that far," I said. "I was in live entertainment."

"Do tell."

"It's not very glamorous. I did some fighting."

"Boxing?"

"Cage."

She thought about that, then shook her head slightly. "I've got to say that doesn't go together in my mind."

"What doesn't?"

"Someone who does that but knows literature and philosophy like you do. But that's a stereotype, isn't it?"

"I don't know," I said. "I never met a pug who could quote Chaucer. On the other hand, I never met a philosopher who could break my nose."

Sophie laughed. Easily. I could have put that laugh around my neck and worn it to the beach, and been happy the rest of the day.

The waitress returned with my coffee. Sophie excused herself and headed for the restroom. I picked up the book she was reading. The book opened at an essay called *John Wayne: A Love Song*. I leafed it. It was about Didion, as a girl, watching John Wayne movies as a girl. Sophie had highlighted this passage:

> And in a world we understood early to be characterized by venality and doubt and paralyzing ambiguities, he suggested another world, one which may or may not have existed ever but in any case existed no more: a place where a man could move free, could make his own code and live by it; a world in which, if a man did what he had to do, he could one day take the girl and go riding through the draw and find

88

himself home free, not in a hospital with something going wrong inside, not in a high bed with flowers and the drugs and the forced smiles, but there at the bend in the bright river, the cottonwoods shimmering in the early morning sun.

SOPHIE CAME BACK and I put the book down.

"Caught me," I said.

"She's a good writer," Sophie said.

"Who else do you like?"

"Jane Austen, of course," Sophie said. "More contemporary, there's—"

A voice said, "What's up?"

Standing there was a guy in very good shape, about my size, six-three. He was staring at Sophie, didn't make a move to look my way.

"What are you doing here?" Sophie said.

"What are *you* doing here?" he said.

The boyfriend alert system went off in my brain.

"I'm having lunch with a friend from the store," Sophie said. "Mike, this is Josh."

I put out my hand.

He left me hanging.

"Can we talk later?" Sophie said.

"How about now?" Josh said.

At this point, the script called for me to offer a warning in a John Wayne voice. *Didn't you hear the lady? Now why don't you mosey on out of here?*

But Sophie looked embarrassed enough. I gazed into my coffee cup.

"Later, please," Sophie said.

I didn't need to look up to know that Josh was using his eyes to burn holes in my head. I took a sip of coffee.

And then he was gone.

"I'm so sorry," Sophie said.

"You don't have to be," I said.

"It's complicated."

"These things usually are," I said. "And I don't want to make things any harder, but ..."

She looked at me, waiting.

"They're going to be," I said. "Because I want to keep seeing you."

I COULDN'T BELIEVE I blurted that out. I half expected her to run screaming from the restaurant.

She did not run, nor did she scream.

She blushed. And with that, without guile or intent, she had me.

We ate, talked about books and theatre and movies and even a little philosophy. Turns out she got hooked on the history of thought by reading her grandfather's copy of Durant's *The Story of Philosophy.* I told her my father had given me a copy when I was a boy, and that got me going on it, too.

She was also an athlete, played volleyball undergrad at San Diego State. Was training for a triathlon.

It was two hours of absolute, unrestricted human normalcy.

When we finished, I could tell she was still thinking about the Josh thing. I was not going to pressure her. I needed time to think myself.

But I did tell her I wanted to do this again.

She said she did, too.

And we shook hands.

Shook. Hands.

I do not know what the current etiquette is. I never did know. The ways of modern romance are a locked-room mystery to me. Maybe someday I'll find the key.

I WAS ALMOST to the Hollywood Bowl on the 101 freeway when Ira called.

"Where are you?" he said.

"Almost to the Bowl," I said.

"Well turn around and come back. The police are here."

"What's going on?"

"They want to talk to you. About that woman you went to see yesterday, Desiree Parks?"

"What about her?"

"She got beaten up," Ira said. "And somebody at the building gave a pretty fair description of you."

I took the Highland off-ramp and got back on the 101 going the other way.

At Ira's I pulled into the driveway. A newly buffed Crown Victoria was parked at the curb.

Ira was in the living room with a man and a woman, who stood when I walked in.

"Detectives Baker and Molina," Ira said.

The man, forty or so, good shape, had gray eyes and the crow's feet of a veteran cop. He shook my hand. "Vic Baker," he said. "This is my partner, Soledad Molina."

Her grip was stronger than her partner's. She was early thirties, had sharp brown eyes and wore a beige suit with creases that could cut meat. She didn't say a word, or smile. She nodded once. It would have been a head-butt had I been any closer.

Baker said, "You were with Desiree Parks yesterday?"

"I was," I said. "How did that information get to you, if I might ask?"

"Mr. Rosen's card was in her purse," he said.

I said, "Was her wallet in the purse?"

"Why do you ask?"

"To see if it was robbery or not."

Baker and Molina exchanged a glance.

Ira smiled.

"Does not appear to be robbery," Baker said. "Let's sit down and you can tell us what happened."

So I told them about meeting Brooklyn Christie, about her father hiring me to find her, about my chat with Desiree and all she told me.

"What time did you leave the location?" Molina asked. It was the first time she'd spoken. Her words were rapid fire. I started to think Rapid Fire would be a good nickname for her.

"About three or so," I said. "How bad is she?"

"She's in a coma," Molina said.

That made me mad. Because I was probably the cause of it. Somebody following or watching. Yes, it could have been a big coincidence, but I wasn't going to make that my working theory.

Baker said, "Do you have any idea who might have wanted to hurt her?"

"None," I said. "I only just met her. She did seem a little defensive."

"In what way?"

"Not trusting me. She had some pepper spray on her key ring. She was ready to use it."

"What was her demeanor like when you left her?" Molina asked.

"She seemed relieved," I said.

"You were described by one of the neighbors," Baker said.

"Which one?"

"We can't tell you that, of course."

"Because I didn't see anybody else," I said. "Oh, except a kid with a periscope."

"Periscope?"

"Security for the building."

Ira looked at me and shook his head, like I shouldn't be joking around.

"Can you account for your time after left the apartment?" Baker said.

"I drove back to the beach," I said. "Then I watched the sun go down."

"Did you talk to anybody?"

"I had an internal dialogue," I said.

"What do you mean?" Molina asked.

"Talking to myself," I said.

Molina said, "So you don't have anyone who can say where you were between three and five yesterday?"

"I have me, and I just told you," I said. "And that's all I'm going to tell you."

Molina looked like she wanted to say something with even more punch behind it, but Baker stopped her by taking out a card and giving it to me. "If anything comes up, you hear anything, will you call me?"

"Anything relevant," I said.

The two detectives stood and Baker thanked Ira.

Nobody thanked me.

Soledad Molina did give me a good-bye nod, though. And that one definitely would have crushed my nose.

"WHY DO YOU antagonize the poor police?" Ira said.

"Can I help my pleasing personality?"

"You will need them someday."

"Just like I need you," I said.

"Cue the violins."

"I mean it. I need your expert legal opinion."

"On what?"

"Breaking and entering," I said.

"It's better not to do both at once," Ira said.

"I want to get into Brooklyn's apartment."

"And just how do you propose to do that?"

"Come on, Ira. Picking a simple lock?"

"No better than a common burglar!"

"But if I get her father's permission, it's not a crime, right?"

Ira folded his arms across his chest. That's his analytical pose. Don't ever get in the way of his analytical pose.

"At most it's criminal trespass," Ira said, "which is not a felony. You would not have the consent of the resident, but of her father. Now, her father no longer has parental authority, so the consent is a little tenuous. He would of course be prepared to testify that he was concerned for his daughter's safety. It's not a rock-solid defense for you, but I'm sure it's enough that the D.A. would not file."

"And what if they did?" I said. "Would you defend me?"

"I'd see that you were sent up the river."

"L.A. doesn't have a river."

"Sure it does. It's just that it's made out of concrete now. Sort of like your head."

"You're the greatest lawyer of all time," I said.

THAT NIGHT I called Ray Christie and filled him in on my conversation with Desiree Parks. I asked him if he'd ever heard his daughter talk about the archangel Michael. He said no and asked me what that was about. He was a man grasping at the meager straws I was holding out. I tried not to let him get his hopes up too high.

It's a tricky thing, hope. If you let it soar too far it can end up like the Hindenburg. Yet most people can't live without hope. I've tried.

I asked his permission to get into Brooklyn's apartment. He said yes, and he wanted to be there. I told him I'd set it up.

Then I decided to watch a movie. I hadn't for a long time. Ira had a set of DVDs in his mobile home, most of them classics. I scanned the titles and decided on a John Wayne. Since Sophie had just read about him, maybe I could find more common ground with the Duke between us.

The movie was *Angel and the Badman*.

I didn't get the chance to start it.

C DOG KNOCKED on my screen door.

"How's it goin'?" he said.

"Just about to watch a movie," I said, stretched out on the sofa. "You want to come in?"

He came in, sliding the door closed behind him.

"Any luck with my guitar?" he said.

"Not yet," I said. "I've had a few other things I needed to do."

"Oh, man."

"Sit down."

He plopped on the futon.

"I'll look into it, C," I said. "How's the other part of our agreement going?"

"Huh?"

"You know, staying clean."

"I'm clean. Totally."

"Really?"

"Yeah, man."

"Would you be willing to pee in a cup?"

His eyes flashed. "You the frickin' cops or something?"

"Just a humble investigator, investigating."

With a sigh, C Dog said, "So what if I smoke a little? A *little*."

"That wasn't our agreement."

"But I like it, man! Keeps me loose. You should try it."

"I get loose with wisdom. I want you to try that."

"Let me get this straight," he said, rubbing his eyes, which were a little red to begin with. "Are you telling me not to smoke at all, and if I do, you're not going to help me get my guitar back?"

"How about you give me a week? What's your favorite junk food?"

"Uh, I don't know, Funyuns?"

"You stock up on Funyuns. When you want to smoke, eat Funyuns instead. For a week. You'll be the picture of health."

"I could try that. But you gotta get me back my guitar."

"I will give it my attention, C. Now how about a lesson in manhood?"

"Manhood?"

"Watch a John Wayne movie with me. I'll make some popcorn."

"Who's John Wayne?"

The decline of Western Civilization was almost complete.

"You're going to find out," I said. "And there will be a quiz afterward."

"Oh, man!"

NEXT MORNING, AROUND ten, I drove Spinoza back to Brooklyn's apartment building. Ray Christie didn't have a key, and gave me permission over the phone to get in any which way I could. I told him to meet me there at eleven.

Picking a simple lock is easy. I'd assembled my own set of tools modeled after Joey Feint's kit—nine picks and three tension wrenches in a leather pouch.

I was inside in ten seconds.

Stuffy was the smell. Nonuse was the tell. It was like a resort cabin in the off season. Dust had settled. The windows were closed with curtains drawn.

On a black, metal-frame coffee table sat a decorative gourd. At least I assumed it wasn't there to be chomped. It was pear-shaped and yellow with black stripes and warts all over. Could have been someone's idea of natural beauty. Or a witch's head.

Next to it was a *People* magazine. The magazine's date was three weeks earlier. There was a sofa with a throw blanket on it, and two bistro-style, retro chairs arranged at either side of the coffee table. On the wall above the sofa was a framed print of Marilyn Monroe standing over the subway grate and holding down her dress.

The small kitchen had a four-burner gas stove and a mid-sized refrigerator. Inside the refrigerator were some Tupperware containers of different shapes, a carton of organic milk, a resealable plastic bag of Bob's Red Mill flaxseeds, and a jar of sunflower seed butter. The vegetable drawer had green plastic bag of spinach which was now soggy and useless. A single, lonely carrot looked like it had crawled into the drawer to die.

I started looking around for anything written—a list, a set of phone numbers, notes-to-self. Nothing in the kitchen.

Down the hallway I peeked in the bathroom and all seemed as it should be. A pink-handled toothbrush sat in a happy-face toothbrush holder on the tile by the mirror. A barely used tube of Earthpaste Lemon Twist Natural Toothpaste was on the side of the porcelain sink.

The only bedroom was at the end of the hall. The door was wide open, the room neat. The queen-sized bed was covered with a light-blue comforter. Two throw pillows with Aztec design covers were on top of the comforter. Between the pillows was a stuffed animal, one of the wild things from Maurice Sendak's book.

I heard something click. Like a door closing.

I listened.

"I'm loaded!" a voice said. Man's voice.

"Hold on there," I said. "I'm a friend of Brooklyn's."

"Come out and show yourself,"

What was this? Tombstone?

"Take it easy," I said. "Here I come."

I walked out of the bedroom and saw him at the end of the hall. He was fat, fortyish, and frizzy of hair. He looked like a guy who should be running a comic book store with live hand grenades under the counter.

He had a single-barrel shotgun in his hands.

It was pointed at me.

"POINT THAT BOOM stick at the ground," I said.

"You just come right out here, slow."

Definitely Tombstone.

I said, "I'm not gonna mosey nowhere with steel on me, podner."

"You do what I tell you!"

"That thing's going to go off, and it will be murder, and it will stain your soul forever," I said. "Point the gun at the floor and listen to me."

"Shut up!"

I leaned against the wall.

"You're going to do some talking to the police," he said.

"You called the police?" I said.

"You bet I called the police. This is my building and you broke in."

"The cops are going to love that you pulled a shotgun on me."

"They will."

"What's your name?" I said.

"You just shut your mouth."

"I'm Mike. I am looking for Brooklyn Christie. She's missing."

"You said you were her friend."

"I am."

"You're a liar," he said.

I was getting real tired of Tombstone. I started visualizing some moves to take away the weapon, remove the shell, and give the man a much-needed enema.

"All right," I said. "Let's wait for the cops. When they get here and figure this out, I want a full apology from you."

He looked like I'd asked him to run naked through a mall.

"Say what?" he said.

"An admission of wrongdoing and a plea for forgiveness," I said.

"You get nothin' from me."

"That will only hurt you," I said. "What's your name?"

"None of your business."

"Well, None, I'm glad we had this chance to talk. This may be the best thing that's ever happened to you."

The shotgun trembled in his hands.

I said, "In one of his dialogues, Plato has Socrates in conversation with a young man named Charmides. Your name isn't Charmides by any chance, is it?"

"I just want you to shut your mouth."

"The police will be here soon. Until then, we ought to redeem the time."

"I don't know what the h—"

"As I was saying, in this dialogue, Socrates talks about the virtue of temperance. He says to Charmides that when temperance is implanted in the soul, health is also imparted, not only to the head, but to the whole body. Now wouldn't that be a nice thing for you to consider?"

"I might just shoot you to shut you up! Be quiet!"

"See? You're being rash, not temperate. And that's just not a good way to live. You never want to angry up your blood, as a famous man once said. Ever heard of Satchel Paige?"

He shook his head. At least he was listening now. Maybe I could even get through to the guy and lull him into a false sense of security. Then I'd sit on him until the cops arrived.

"Satchel Paige was a famous pitcher, in the old Negro Leagues. One of the greatest of all time. He was in his late forties when the color barrier was broken."

My captor lowered the gun barrel. Just a little.

Heck, maybe I could put the guy to sleep.

"What is it you do for a living, Charmides?" I said.

"Please, just be quiet, will you?"

The gun drooped a bit more.

I took one small step, talking as I did. "Let me offer you a free piece of advice."

"Please don't."

"*Homo sum humani a me nihil alienum puto.*"

He just stared.

"It means," I said, "I am human, thus nothing human is alien to me. You see?"

"I hate you."

"No, I am alien to you, but I'm just like you. A man. A human being. We should be able to reach some meeting of the minds without a gun between us."

He sighed. He shook a little.

I took one more step.

And the shotgun went *BOOM.*

PRIOR TO ARISTOTLE, philosophy held, by and large, that

there is no intentionality in nature. Random events are just that. No point. Thus, a stone rolling down a hill not only gathers no moss, it doesn't have any meaning in the larger order of things. And never will.

This did not satisfy Aristotle, who sought causes and explanations for everything.

Epicurus, on the other hand, taught that everything was the result of the random collisions of atoms. Therefore life was only "unfair" to those trying to impose a moral order that does not exist.

But there is something about getting shot that cries out for not only for an explanation, but retribution.

After the shotgun blast, the pellets made nasty work of the hall carpet just inches from my feet. But several, following the laws of physics, bounced off the hardwood underneath the carpet and ricocheted into my shins. One of the pellets ripped my pants at my left knee. A little higher and more to the middle and my dangling participle would have been severely edited.

Which didn't do a whole lot for my calmness of spirit.

The guy with the now-empty shotgun had a shocked look on his face. I knew he hadn't intended to fire, but motive was not a concern to me. This was not a court of law. This was the court of Romeo.

I pounced.

The man whipped the shotgun up, butt out. But the fear in his eyes signaled the onset of our body's fight-or-flight system. His peripheral blood vessels were contracting, and his muscles were bathed in adrenal and cortisol juices, tightened.

That was all I needed to stop the butt with the palm of my left hand and, with my right coming up on the barrel from below, rip the shotgun from him.

My legs burned. I threw the shotgun behind me.

"Ouch!" I said. "That hurt!"

"I ... I didn't mean ..."

He tried to turn then and make for the door.

I grabbed his shirt and pulled him back and put my hand behind his neck. A squeeze and a simple takedown later, he was on the floor face down.

"Don't hurt me!" he muffled into the carpet.

"You idle-headed pignut!" I said, channeling Shakespeare. I sat on his back and took stock of my jeans. There was some blood.

"You're not gonna kill me, are you?" the man said.

"Let me think about it," I said.

"Please get off me."

"Let me think about that, too."

THE COPS ARRIVED five minutes later. Only now they thought they had a shooting on their hands. The blast from the shotgun must have alerted some of the neighbors, who met the black-and-white SUV that rolled up.

A voice from the squad vehicle loudspeaker said, "This is Los Angeles police. Put your weapons down and put your hands on the back of your head, and come out of the door walking backwards."

"Now look what you've done," I said to my human cushion.

"I'm so sorry," he said.

"Stay on the floor."

I got up and picked up the shotgun. I went to the apartment door and opened it.

"Coming out!" I shouted.

Then I slid the shotgun outside.

I put my hands behind my head and kicked the door all the way open.

Just before I backed out I said, "Read the novel *Crime and Punishment* by Dostoevsky. Got that? *Crime and Punishment*. Read the whole thing. I'm going to come back someday and give you a quiz on it. If you haven't read it, I'm going to break your nose."

The man on the floor looked at me with a genuine, existential fear.

My job was done.

I backed out of the door.

THEY CUFFED ME and the shooter, put us in separate squad cars. Just as we pulled away from the scene, I saw Ray Christie drive up, get out of his car, and look confused. He reminded me of mankind itself, stumbling through the ages looking for answers.

At the station, a senior patrol officer named Martins took my statement. I gave him my version of the events. His eyebrows went up every so often.

When I finished, he left the interview room and another officer, this one a sergeant, came in. His name was Rice. He looked seasoned.

"We're going to change things up a little, Mr. Romeo. I'm going to give you the Miranda advisement."

"Consider it done," I said. "You have a waiver?"

Rice slid a form to me. I signed it.

"Ask away," I said.

"Why did you break into Brooklyn Christie's apartment?"

"As I told Officer Martins, I have been retained to find her. I work for a lawyer, Ira Rosen. Brooklyn's father wants to find his daughter. I asked him for permission to unlock the door of Brooklyn's apartment, and he gave it to me."

"Unlock is a funny word, don't you think?"

"I'm going to want my lock pick set back, by the way."

"Right now it's potential evidence," Rice said. "Is her father on the lease?"

"You can find out," I said.

"Will you give us his contact information?"

"No, I will not."

He gave me the cop glare. I gave him the Romeo.

"You're not going to make this easy on us?" Rice said.

"I'm making it very easy," I said. "I've given you a statement that is absolutely true and correct. That's all you need to know. You want to issue a misdemeanor citation, go ahead. But I'll make you show up in court and explain yourself to the judge. You can tell him why you held and questioned a gunshot victim."

"Do you need medical attention, Mr. Romeo?"

"I could use a thick steak. With onions."

Rice wrote something down. Then put down his pen and folded his hands. "You had contact with a Desiree Parks, did you not?"

"What's this about?"

"Just answer the question."

"I already went through this with a detective named Baker," I said.

"Go through it with me," Rice said.

"I don't want to."

Rice shook his head. "Okay, Mr. Romeo, have it your way. The law says we can hold you for forty-eight hours pending further investigation."

"I want to call my lawyer."

"Certainly, Mr. Romeo."

"And I'm serious about that steak."

THEY HAD A cell for me, complete with a roomie.

He wore his hoodie full up. He looked like a novitiate in a monastery. He sat cross-legged on his bunk, head down, as if praying.

I started doing some push-ups against the cell bench when I heard him say, "Hey."

I stopped, turned, sat on the bench. "What's up?" I said.

"What are you doing?"

"Push-ups."

"Why?"

"Keep in shape," I said.

"What you here for?"

"Contempt of cop," I said.

"I hear that."

"How about you?" I said.

"Assault."

"Did you?"

He gave me a long look from within his cowl. "What are you sayin'?"

"Just asking the question."

"You try to fight me, I'll make you feel it," he said. "You wanna try me?"

"I don't like fighting."

"Somebody burn me, he gonna pay."

"You looked like you were praying just now," I said.

"So?"

"It's good to have something to believe in," I said. "Besides fighting."

"So somebody hurt you, you just do nothin' about it?"

It was a good question, the right question.

"If someone is doing something bad," I said, "it's moral to stop him with equal force. But we shouldn't be the ones to start it."

The monk said, "Man, who are you?"

"Mike." I put out my hand.

He shook it. "Richard." He sounded like a teenager.

"You got anybody looking out for you?" I said. "Mom, dad?"

"My mom's done with me," he said.

"Does she have a case?"

"What?"

"Have you done things that make her want to be done with you?"

"You don't know nothin' about it."

"Why I'm asking."

Richard shrugged. "Sometimes I get mad. So what?"

"Getting mad's easy," I said. "Controlling your wrath is the hard part."

"My what?"

"Wrath."

"What's that?"

"Ever heard of Achilles?" I said.

"Who?"

I said, "Let me tell you about him." And I did. Complete with commentary and annotations, which included references to the life of one Michael Romeo. The kid listened to the whole thing. Which was a good sign. Here I was in a jail cell and I felt a little charge of hope. Crazy. This starfish business was getting to me.

IRA ARRIVED A little after one. Ray Christie was with him. After Ray gave a statement, and Ira sweet-talked the cops a little, they asked me if I wanted to file a charge against the guy with the shotgun. I waved it off. "Just tell him to take a fire-arms safety course," I said.

Then I was sprung.

Outside the station, Ray Christie seemed shaken. "I never thought you'd get shot," he said. "I'm so sorry!"

"Part of the job, Ray," I said.

"The police wouldn't let me go into the apartment," Ray said.

"It doesn't look like anybody's been there for awhile," I said.

Ray Christie let out a deep, despairing breath.

"The police are involved now," Ira said to Ray.

"I know how that goes," Ray said. "Overworked and underpaid. Missing persons aren't their top priority."

"It's mine," I said.

"YOU'RE A TROUBLE magnet, you know that?" Ira said. He was driving me back to the apartment building so I could pick up Spinoza, who was parked on the street there.

"Some people are born with that gift," I said.

"Is it your inner Achilles that makes you rude to people, including the police?"

"Funny you should mention that," I said. "I was just giving a lecture."

"Don't fool with me, Michael."

"No fooling. An audience of one, in my cell."

"You had a cellie?"

"Richard. He's got a P.D., but I thought maybe you could take a look at his case."

"You volunteered me?"

"I told him what a great guy you were," I said.

"*Pro bono?*"

"I know that's what you love," I said. "Merciful to the poor and all that. Plus, he's a good kid. How about talking to him?"

Ira sighed. "Who is working for who around here?"

"I love you, too," I said.

"How are your legs?" he said.

"A little bruised. Hole in my jeans. But my pride is intact."

"You could have had some valuable machinery messed up. God must be watching over you."

"Or I'm just lucky," I said.

"You can believe that if you want to," Ira said.

"We all believe what we want to."

Ira shook his head. "I don't want to believe I am a sin-filled man, but I must."

"You're the least sin-filled man I know," I said. "But that doesn't make you any less annoying."

"Spoken like a guilty client who's mad he didn't walk."

"Pull over," I said. "We're here."

My car was sitting at the curb. The excitement of the day had long since died out. Ira told me to get in my car and drive away. I promised him I would.

I did not tell him *when* I would. Lawyers aren't the only people who can work loopholes into an agreement.

Sitting on Spinoza's hood, I leveled my eyes at the complex. A little like Superman and his X-ray vision. Somebody in there had seen the attacker. Had given a description that was somewhat similar to me.

It could have come from the building next door. There were windows that looked out at the common driveway and Desiree's front door. The two upstairs windows of the building were shut. One had closed venetian blinds, the other closed curtains.

It occurred to me I could canvass the place. Knock knock. *Hi, I'm the guy who threw the shotgun out the door earlier today. Can I have a word?*

Why the heck not? The worst they could do is scream and get another shotgun.

I started with the four units in the other building. Two of the apartments didn't answer my knock. One downstairs did. It was an elderly woman who thought I was trying to sell her magazines. She looked at me through thick glasses and told me she wasn't born yesterday.

That I believed.

One of the upstairs apartments had a smallish man of around forty who kept a chain on his door as he opened it a crack.

"There was some excitement next door," I said. "Did you get questioned by the police?"

He shook his head.

"Did you see what happened earlier today?"

He shook his head.

I was reminded of those three monkeys.

I thanked him and told him to stay vigilant.

Then I went across to Brooklyn's building, to the door of the lower apartment on the other side. I wondered where the guy with the shotgun was. I wondered if they'd taken away his weapon. I wondered if I should be here at all.

I knocked.

A woman's voice asked who it was.

"The guy who almost got shot today," I said.

Not a normal greeting, I know.

"What do you want?" the woman said.

"I'm trying to talk to anybody who might have seen the man who hurt your neighbor, Desiree Parks."

Long pause.

"Please go away," she said.

I thought I heard a voice, a smaller voice—a child?—in the background. Then the woman's voice saying, "Be quiet."

"I work for a lawyer," I said, which was becoming my new mantra. It was the only thing that gave me a whiff of legitimacy.

I heard the small voice again.

Then the woman. "Would you mind backing away from the door?"

"Sure." I took two steps backward.

The woman opened the door and stepped out. She was around thirty, I guessed, black, wearing blue jeans and a red, pullover blouse.

And she was not alone.

Holding her hand was a boy, probably eight. He was in jeans and a Rams T-shirt and tennis shoes.

"My son says you talked to him before," the woman said.

It clicked. To the boy I said, "Are you the security guy, with the periscope?"

The boy nodded.

"We did talk," I said to the mom. "I'm an investigator, trying to find one of your neighbors, Brooklyn."

"I know her name."

"Do you also know Desiree?"

The woman nodded.

"Someone beat her up," I said. Off her look, I added, "It wasn't me."

"I know," she said.

"You know?"

"Better come inside," she said.

THE WOMAN CLOSED the door and faced me.

"I don't know what's going on," she said, "but I want it to stop."

"I'm not sure what's going on either," I said. "And I want to find out. May I know your name?"

"I'd rather not say," she said.

"Okay," I said.

"I mean, I know how this can go down."

"You're afraid of retaliation."

She nodded.

"I get it," I said. "I won't reveal anything you tell me."

"Not even to the police?"

"Not even."

"You said you're investigating?"

I took an Ira lawyer card out and gave it to her. "This is the lawyer I work for. We're trying to locate Brooklyn. When I came here I met Desiree, and talked to her. Then today a crazy man fired a shotgun at me."

"Mr. Stalboerger," she said. "He's a piece of work. Is that how come your pants are ripped?"

"A little ventilation," I said. "It could've been worse."

The boy said, "Tell him."

The mother said, "Eric was using his periscope out the window. He saw a big man go into Desiree's apartment, and then come out later."

"A big man?" I said.

The boy nodded.

"How big?" I asked.

"Like you," the boy said.

"Did you notice anything else about him?" I said.

The boy tugged on his mother's sweater, motioned for her to bend down. When she did, he whispered something in her ear.

She straightened up. "He had dark skin. Not like yours."

The boy tugged again, the mother listened again.

"He had a picture on his arm," she said. "I guess he means a tattoo. He says it was a dog in a hat."

A little memory flashed. "Do you have a computer or tablet handy?"

There was a laptop on the kitchen table. The mom gave me permission to do a search. I typed in *USMC bulldog tattoo* and came up with a page of images. With Eric at my side I scrolled slowly. He stopped me and pointed to one.

"That one," he said.

I stood. "That's all I need. Thank you. You've been a great help. And everything we've done is confidential."

I put out my hand for the boy. We shook.

"Good work, Eric," I said.

The woman offered her hand to me. "My name's Lynette," she said.

WE ALL CARRY monsters around inside us. One of the main questions philosophy asks is, can we kill our monsters? If not, can we tame them?

I was thinking about that as I drove away from Brooklyn's building. I knew, the way farmers sense a storm coming, that I'd better be prepared to exercise some serious self-control. Because I was burning to have a talk with a certain bartender at Kahuna's.

Which is why I decided to head to a boxing gym in the Valley. Jimmy's is a traditional prizefighting space. I discovered it shortly after getting to L.A. It's a place I can go and work on the heavy bag, the speed bag, jump a little rope, work up a sweat and watch the younger fighters going through their paces.

I had some gym clothes in the back of my car. I checked out a pair of mitts at the counter and went over to start on the heavy bag. Jimmy's has a boxing ring in the middle, and workout stations all around.

I'd been giving the bag something to think about for five minutes when Jimmy himself came over.

Jimmy Sarducci is a short, stocky, third-generation Italian-American who was a Golden Gloves flyweight champion back in the day. He's gotten a little large around the belt, but his gray hair is thick and held in the grip of about half a canister of mousse.

We greeted each other and I kept at the bag. Jimmy does that, wanders the gym and watches the guys—and the occasional woman—as they work out.

After I peppered a few more punches, Jimmy said, "You got the look."

"The look?" I said.

"You are a Greek god."

I snorted and hit the bag with a solid right.

"Which one?" I said.

Jimmy cocked his head.

"There's a whole pantheon of Greek gods," I said. "Which one do you think I am?"

"It's just a way of talking," Jimmy said. "I don't know from Greek gods. One of those guys throwing lightning or something?"

"That would be Zeus. He's the king. But he's a jerk. I don't want to be Zeus."

"I don't really care who—"

"Then there's Heracles."

"There's who?"

Bap, bap. A combination. I said, "Heracles is the Greek name for Hercules. I don't want to be Heracles either, because he was only half a god and he was a jerk, too."

"All I was talking about—"

"What about Hermes? Now he was a smart kid. They say that by noon of the day he was born he crawled right out of his cradle and invented the lyre."

"What'd he lie about?"

"The lyre is a stringed instrument, Jimmy. Hermes was a herald, a messenger, and had wings on his heels. That would be something good for a boxer to have, wouldn't it?"

"I think so, but I'm—"

"I don't want to be a Greek god at all, Jimmy. I go for the Norse. If I have to be somebody, let it be Thor."

"I saw that movie!"

Pop, pop, pop. Right, left, right to the bag. "I'm not talking about some Hollywood beefcake. I'm talking about the real Thor. The guy with the hammer. The god of thunder."

"Wait a minute!" Jimmy said. "That's how I'll bill you. The Hammer!"

I stopped punching. "Bill me?"

"When you fight for me," Jimmy said.

"You want to manage me?"

He grabbed my wrist. "Make a fist," he said.

I did.

He held my fist in the air. "That's your hammer."

"Let me finish my workout, Jimmy, and then maybe we can talk."

I had no intention of fighting for anyone.

"Okay, Hammer," Jimmy said.

I DID ANOTHER twenty minutes on the heavy bag. Jumped rope for ten minutes, did some push-ups and crunches.

Midway through the crunch set something occurred to me. When I was done I grabbed a towel off the shelf and ran it over my face and arms then hung it around my neck. I went over to the ring where Jimmy was watching a couple of young fighters pretend they were raging bulls.

"There he is," Jimmy said. "The Hammer!"

"Can we step into your office a minute?" I said.

"To sign a contract?"

"You may not want to manage me after you hear me out."

"There's nothing you can say to me that would get me to forget we have invented a legend here."

"Your office, please."

Jimmy's office was cubical size. Every square inch of wall was covered with photographs of boxers, framed items from newspapers, a few motivational sayings done in fancy font and held up by yellowing tape:

Keep punching. You always have a puncher's chance.

Defeat is not when you fall. It's when you don't stand up again.

Work hard, think fast—and then you'll last.

Jimmy's desk was a sea of detritus. Stacks of papers, fight

magazines, nubs of pencils—I liked it that somebody still used pencils. Jimmy sat behind the desk, settling into a squeaky, wooden executive-type chair, something you would've found in a lawyer's office around 1954.

The only other furniture in the place was a corner stool from a fight ring. I sat on it, sinking to Jimmy's eye level.

"So what do we have to talk about?" he said.

"How long you been in the fight game in L.A.?" I said.

"Oh, thirty years now," he said. "I came out from New Jersey to be a consultant on a boxing movie that Mickey Rourke was gonna do. But he couldn't get it funded. I decided I liked the warm weather and set down some roots. Also there were some guys in Jersey wanted to kill me, so it seemed like a good time to start over."

"Kill you?"

Jimmy shrugged. "Sometimes in this business you get on the wrong side of people. Blame it on the Bossa Nova."

"The who?"

"You remember the song, don't you?"

"What song?"

"Blame it on the Bossa Nova," he said. "Eydie Gormé."

"Before my time," I said.

"My time is your time," he said. "What's up?"

"You've probably run into a lot of muscle," I said. "The kind who do things to people for a price."

Jimmy leaned toward me. His chair squeaked like a haunted house door. "I don't know if I like where this is going."

"It hasn't gone anywhere yet," I said.

"Keep punching."

"I work for a lawyer."

"I'm sorry."

"And I'm looking for a woman."

"Join the club."

"A woman who's gone missing," I said. "There's a punk who beat up another woman, a neighbor of the missing one, and I want to know why. I thought I might ask if you know anything about a bartender in Malibu by the name of Kalolo."

Jimmy steepled his fingers and looked at one wall of fight photos.

After a beat or two, he looked back t me and said, "I got your word this conversation stays here?"

"You've got my word," I said.

" 'Cause to most people, word don't mean jack. I still got some honor. I want to know if you got honor."

"Aristotle said the two greatest virtues were courage and honor."

"Aristotle, huh?" Jimmy smiled. "He ever go back on his word?"

"He always paid his toga bills on time. You have my word that this conversation remains confidential."

"I'm gonna trust you then. But don't stick me. You do, I never forget."

"Fair deal," I said.

Jimmy picked up one of the nubby pencils and started bouncing the eraser end on his desk. "I don't know the name of this guy that you just said. But I know a guy who might know a guy who might know. Only this guy, the guy who might know, he doesn't like to be asked questions. There's got to be something in it for him of a monetary nature."

"How monetary?"

"Four or five yards."

"The return on that investment is too risky," I said. "But maybe we can barter something."

"Like what?"

"I have no idea. Maybe the guy could use some legal advice. I think it would be worth a meeting."

"You want me to try to set something up?"

"It would be mighty nice of you, Jimmy."

"And you want to find this bartender, right?"

"I already know where the bartender is. What I want to know is if he works for someone."

Jimmy ran his hand over his face. He had the knuckles of an ex-fighter. Gnarled, like a row of walnuts.

"I'll arrange something," he said, "but what do you give me? Let's talk about that little arrangement."

"How about a big hug?"

"How about you fight for me?"

"Jimmy, you can't be serious. You want somebody who's younger and will be around a while, who you can develop."

"You seen the tomato cans I got around here? Guy who looks like you, shaped like you, you're box office, baby. The fans you could draw!"

"I don't do things for fans."

"The money would be killer."

"How about you arrange this meeting, and then we'll have this conversation again?"

"You give me your word on that?"

"You have my word."

"Bossa Nova," he said. "I'll see what I can do."

AT A LITTLE after ten the next morning I drove up to Kahuna's. I parked on PCH and put on my Dodgers hat and kept on my shades. I crossed the street and went in through the far door that takes you directly to Kahuna's outdoor patio where there's self seating. Here you can sit and watch the ocean through a Plexiglas wind barrier as you sip your beer and make movie deals. Or dream of making them.

And if you get the right table, you can also see inside to the bar area.

I selected the right table.

A waitress came over and placed some silverware wrapped inside a paper napkin on my table, along with a menu. She asked if I'd like something to drink. I ordered a Corona.

Kalolo was at the bar, jawing with a customer. ESPN was on the TV. The sun was shining on the sea.

The waitress returned with my Corona. I pushed the lime wedge through the bottle opening, put my thumb on the top, and turned the bottle upside down. The lime floated upward. I turned the bottle back over and let the fizz out by slowly releasing my thumb.

It made a refreshing hiss. We all need our rituals.

I sipped and watched Kalolo work the bar. A guy came in and sat at the corner. He looked faux low-pro. That's a celeb who dresses up to look low profile. He usually has a two-day shadow, faded jeans, and a T-shirt that is supposed to look casual but is somehow without a wrinkle. And a baseball hat worn straight. The backward look is so 1999.

This guy had it all.

Kalolo knew him and they exchanged a clumsy dap so they could indulge the illusion of being cool.

I sipped and watched.

I got my fish taco. It was Cajun-crusted with ceviche on top. A few more people had joined me on the patio. The bar stayed pretty much the same.

Then Kalolo stepped out from the bar and headed down the corridor toward the bathrooms. I put a ten dollar bill on the table and followed him.

KALOLO WAS AT a urinal when I entered. I saw that the two stalls had open doors.

We were alone.

He glanced at me.

"Don't let me stop you," I said.

In rather colorful terms, he inquired as to my presence.

"I know about Desiree Parks," I said.

"I don't know what you're talkin' about, man."

Wrong answer. A guy like this, if he really was ignorant, would have told me to do something awful to myself. But there was that hesitation, that little worm of fear wiggling around inside him. He knew I knew the truth now and he could not for the life of him figure out how I knew.

"Got you, Kalolo," I said.

He flushed the toilet. Zipped up. Came toward me.

"Don't forget to wash your hands," I said.

One more step, and then he threw a smoked ham fist at my face. His bigness was not an advantage. The trajectory of his blow had more ground to cover and that hair of a second was all I needed to pull my head back. Pacific Island knuckles breezed past my chin.

My reaction was instant, instinctive, and a setback for American-Polynesian relations. I plowed my fist into his right kidney. Pain burst in his eyes. His groan was deep.

I placed my right hand behind his head and slammed his face into the mirror.

The mirror cracked.

From there it was a simple matter to get him to the floor. I held him down by putting my left knee on the back of his neck and a hammerlock on his arm. With my free hand I removed a thick wallet from his back pocket.

Kalolo moaned.

I was glad Kahuna's preferred loud music. I could hear Billy Joel telling everyone not to worry, 'cause he was all right.

I pulled out the cards he had stuffed in his wallet.

"Mwwaww ..." Kalolo said, his face pressed into the floor.

I held him down.

With my free hand I looked at a well-thumbed card for a

car mechanic. A black-and-gold card for *Kandy's Attic, A Gentlemen's Club*. An *Ace Frozen Yogurt* card with eight holes punched in it. He only had four more to go for a free cup.

Then one that seemed out of place. A neat, white business card.

For Dr. Gary Pasfield, UCLA. The guy from the rally.

Funny, but Kalolo didn't strike me as the scholarly type.

I put the cards back in the wallet and tossed it aside.

"How you doing there, Lightning?" I said.

"Mwawww ..."

I had to get out of there before somebody came in. I said, "I know you put the hurt on Desiree Parks. I can prove you did. So if you want to call the cops, you go ahead and do it. Tell them I'll be watching you from now on."

Kalolo finally managed to say something coherent.

But it was not nice what he said.

I grabbed his hair, pulled his head up, and hammered the bathroom floor with his face.

He went to sleep.

I walked out.

WHEN I GOT back to my place I went into the bathroom. I took some deep breaths and looked at my grill in the mirror.

Cicero believed in *summum bonum,* the "highest good." Plato thought it existed in actual reality somewhere, and our job was to look around down here, in the shadows, and find it. Or at least get as close to it as we can.

All I could think about as I looked at myself in the mirror was, nice try, humanity. You almost made it. But the forces against you are too strong.

I splashed cold water on my face. Then I got a Dos Equis from the refrigerator and sat down with my laptop. A search for Gary Pasfield led me to a UCLA website and this faculty description:

Dr. Gary Pasfield
B.S. in Biological Sciences, University of California at Los Angeles
Ph.D. in Integrative Ecology, University of Cambridge, England

My chief interest is research in biodiversity models, including the elasticity of energy, water, and carbon exchange affecting land surface temperature. My aim is to translate scientific findings into practical information for the guidance of conservation planning, protection of endangered ecosystems, and preservation of the Earth.

THE PAGE TOLD me his office was in the Life Sciences Building on the UCLA campus.

Maybe it was time for me to go back to college.

But before that I had to do some schooling.

Because C Dog was at my door once again.

"Sup?" he said.

"I'm tempted to say *sup* too, but I resist," I said.

"Can I come in?"

"Enter."

He did.

"Got another beer?" he said.

"The refrigerator," I said.

He got the refreshment and sat on my futon.

"Is this just a hanging out visit?" I said. "Because I'm actually working."

"On getting my guitar back?"

"Believe it or not I have other things on my plate."

He took a sip. There was something he wanted to say and he was trying to figure out a way to say it.

"What's on your mind?" I said.

"Nothin'."

"Well there's your problem right there," I said. "You need to have something on your mind. Otherwise, what's it good for? It would be like having a fine guitar that sits in the corner, never gets played."

"Maybe you're right."

"Of course I'm right," I said. "Who do you think you're talking to?"

He smiled.

"But I have a feeling you want to ask me something," I said.

C Dog took a pull on the bottle. He lowered it and held it with both hands, as if it were a crystal ball. "What do you think of suicide?" he said.

I closed my laptop and put it on the coffee table.

"Why are you asking?" I said.

"I just been thinking about it, and you're a thinker," he said.

"Do you have suicidal thoughts?"

He shrugged. "I was just thinking about it is all. I was thinking what's the point of going through all this? Why not check out? How come you stick?"

Out of the mouths of babes. Carter "C Dog" Weeks had managed to ask one of the most profound questions of life, for anybody.

"I stick," I said, "because I want to find out."

"Find out?"

"Why I should stick."

C Dog furrowed his forehead. His gray cells were working hard.

"You get this one life," I said. "Instead of ending it, why not observe it? You'll die eventually. Why not try to find some answers?"

"Maybe there ain't no answers."

"Maybe not. Maybe so. You'll never find out unless you give it a shot."

He took another long drink. "I woke up today and it was the same as yesterday. That's why I get high, man. It gets me through. Now you want to take it away from me. You take that away, what's the point?"

"You want your life to be dependent on a plant?"

"Maybe," he said.

"Give me a year," I said.

"A year for what?"

"You don't think about suicide for a year. We'll mark our calendars. One year from now we'll have another conversation like this. Between now and then, we'll work on things the way we set it up. How's that sound?"

He didn't answer right away. The waves on the beach were louder than usual. Maybe a storm in Mexico feeling its way north.

"Agreed?" I said.

"Maybe," he said.

"Yes or no. And mean it."

With a sigh he said, "Okay. Yeah."

"Now spit in your right hand," I said.

"Whu?"

I spit in mine. "Like that."

"You crazy?"

"Compared to whom?"

Then C Dog laughed, like we were in on a goof together.

He spat in his hand. I got up and went over and put my hand on his and we shook.

"This is a solemn oath," I said.

"It feels frickin' gross."

"That's so you won't forget it," I said. "Now say, I, Carter C Dog Weeks, do solemnly swear not to dwell on thoughts of my own death until one year from today."

He hesitated then repeated the words.

"Any questions?" I said.

"Can I have a paper towel?"

I got us paper towels and wondered where I'd come up with this ritual. Maybe it was an old TV show I'd seen when I was a kid.

"So you think you can find my guitar?" C Dog said.

"I'll work on it," I said. "But if you never got that guitar back, could you accept it and move on?"

"No way!"

"Yes way. You accept that you can deal with the worst and that makes life easier to manage."

The answer didn't please him, but he gave no rejoinder. He got up and put his beer bottle on the coffee table. He moved to the screen door, stopped and turned.

"So what's one thing you've found out?" he said.

"Found out?"

"That makes you think life maybe doesn't suck?"

I was about to give him a flip answer, to avoid going any deeper today. But then it hit me, what I did have going. And it was as clear as a cloudless day on the beach.

"Her name is Sophie," I said.

I'D PLANNED A visit to the UCLA campus to try to collar Dr. Gary Pasfield. According to his schedule, posted online, he had a seminar in the morning. So I took that time to drive all the way to the Argo.

I got there right as the store opened. Not that I was anxious or anything.

Sophie had just unlocked the door. When she saw me she looked surprised.

Then pleased. "Hello," she said.

"I was in the neighborhood," I said.

She played along. "Looking for anything special?"

I'm looking at it.

"Ah, maybe some poetry," I said. "I'm in the mood for verse."

"Sure," she said. "Over on aisle six, the left side toward the end. I'll find you in a little while."

So I wandered over to the poetry section. Scanned the shelf a little. Took down a volume of Theodore Roethke. Turned to his most famous poem, "The Waking." *I wake to sleep, and take my waking slow. I feel my fate in what I cannot fear. I learn by going where I have to go …*

I read the whole thing. It had been twenty years since I'd read it the first time, as a fifteen-year-old Yale sophomore. It knocked me out then, and did the same now.

Right next to Roethke on the shelf was Shel Silverstein. *Where the Sidewalk Ends.* This was a nice collection Argo had going on.

And good old Ovid. He was a Roman poet born in the first century B.C. He's known best for his *Metamorphoses,* which tells entertaining stories about gods and their bizarre interactions with human beings. It was written during the time of Caesar Augustus, when the empire was under heavy taxation and fear of foreign enemies.

The more things change, the more they stay the same.

Ovid wrote fantasy, like telling us how we got echoes. Echo was a nymph who could only repeat the last part of whatever she heard. Her unreturned love for the self-centered Narcissus caused her to waste away in bodily form until only her voice remained.

Narcissists make all of us feel like we're wasting away. And there seem to be more of them all the time.

Scanning for more I caught a collection of the Cavalier poets. Got a nice warmth from that. My mother loved the Cavaliers. She introduced me to them when I was ten and smitten with a girl named Brenda Mumford, with whom I had no chance. Mom gave me some Cavalier poetry. There was romance in it, but also honor and duty and things I wasn't getting much of in school.

I was just turning to a favorite old poem when Sophie tapped me lightly on the shoulder.

"What have you got there?" she said.

I put my thumb in the book to hold the place. "Sir John Suckling," I said. "Poet and the inventor of Cribbage."

"I love Cribbage. But I don't know the poet."

"Ah."

"Which of his do you like?" She put her hand under mine, the one holding the book, and raised it. The wiring in my body started to hum.

She took the book out of my hand, placing her thumb in the place where I'd had mine. She opened the book and looked at the page.

"'The Constant Lover'?" she said.

I nodded.

She began to read out loud:

"*Out upon it! I have loved*
Three whole days together,
And am like to love three more
If it prove fair weather."

She looked at me and said, "That one?"

I answered by putting my arm around her waist.

She came to me willingly, her body soft against mine, and the kiss was warm, brief, sensational.

When we parted, our faces inches from each other, she said, "Wow."

"Is it fair weather?" I said.

"Sunny and warm," she said.

"No sign of rain?"

"Not even clouds."

I kissed her again.

This one lasted longer.

An elderly woman came around the corner and almost bumped into us. Sophie sheepishly smoothed her blouse. The woman smiled.

"You make a lovely couple," she said.

The blush is an involuntary response of the blood vessels, triggered by the brain's release of protective chemicals. I don't know that there is a good evolutionary explanation for the blush, what adaptive advantage it held. All I know is my cheeks were responding as if I were a sophomore.

We were both like that, Sophie and me. We said nothing to the woman because I'm not sure our mouths were working properly. The kiss had melted them.

Finally, Sophie said, "I should get back to the counter."

"When can I see you again?" I said.

"Saturday?"

"Not soon enough."

She laughed. "I think it's the only day, I've got—"

I kissed her quickly.

"Saturday then," I said.

"That's specific enough for me," she said.

I WALKED OUT of the store without buying a book. I can't remember the last time I'd left a bookstore without at least one book under my arm.

It was another perfect day in L.A., as the song says. I went to the coffee house on the corner and bought a dark roast drip.

When I came back out there were three men waiting for me.

One of them was Josh, Sophie's ex. The other two guys were linebacker types. One was white and one was black. They wore tight shirts that showed off their mounds of muscle. If you have to flaunt it, you're already two strikes behind in the count as far as I'm concerned.

"You shouldn't be here," Josh said.

"But I like coffee," I said.

"Not what I mean. You know what I mean."

"Help me out," I said.

"Where Sophie works. Where Sophie is anywhere."

"You stalking your ex-girlfriend?"

"There's three of us," Josh said. "You want it now or you want it later?"

"Here on the street?" I said. "With kids around?"

"Stay away from her," Josh said. "I don't want to see your face around here."

"Don't you think Sophie has a say in this?"

"She's not here."

"Let's go in and talk to her about it," I said.

"Gonna be no talk," Josh said. "You walk away."

I looked at the other two. "You boys play football?"

They tried to make their faces look like bricks. It wasn't a stretch.

"This is between us," Josh said.

"But they might want to avoid career-ending injury, which is what I'll hand out."

The brick-faced ballers tried to look like they weren't concerned.

"I don't want to fight anybody, okay?" I said. "It's not necessary. Let's be prudent about this."

Josh slapped the coffee cup out of my hand.

It hit the sidewalk and exploded.

Hot coffee hit my jeans.

It also splashed on a boy of about four years old. He was just to my right, walking out of the store with his mother. He grabbed his cheek and started to cry.

There was a half second pause when both Josh and I knew what was going to happen next.

WHEN I WAS five I got into my first fight. It was in the play yard at the kindergarten I was attending. A new boy had joined our august company and he seemed to have something I did not. I noticed it immediately, as boys do. It was a confidence, a strength. He was the exact opposite of me.

His name was Dylan.

And I wanted to be him. He was better than everyone at games. He could swing on the bars like a gibbon. The girls flocked around him. My best friend in the school, Owen Palatsi, started playing more with Dylan than he did with me.

Generating feelings I could not yet analyze. All I knew was that I felt abandoned.

I told my mom about it, crying one night that this boy had taken away my best friend and nobody liked me. She tried to talk me down. She did her best.

It didn't take.

One day at school I was out in the yard playing with a fire truck, rolling it on the ground by myself, when Dylan came running by and snatched it up with one hand.

"Give it back!" I did not shout it, I screamed it. Even then I knew it was an overreaction. A red cloud covered me as I got to my feet.

Dylan stopped and laughed.

Normally, a situation of such obvious schoolyard injustice

would have been handled by one of the aides. But for some reason today's helper was on the other side of the yard. I think Fate was experimenting on me for the first time.

"Give it!" I said.

"I just want to look at it," Dylan said.

"It's mine!"

This is also how the Trojan War began.

When he did not give me the fire engine, I unleashed all the anger that had been building up inside me. It came out in my wildly swinging arms. I threw fists at his body, but the blows lacked power. Throaty screams made sounds in me I'd never heard before.

When I'd softly landed seven or eight of these feather-duster punches, Dylan dropped the fire engine and put one of his hands on my face—it seemed the size of a catcher's mitt—and pushed.

My head snapped back and I fell on my butt.

Flames erupted and I knew for the first time what blind rage was. I don't even remember getting on my feet, but the next thing I knew, with tears pouring out of my eyes, I was standing in the time-out corner of the yard with the aide, Ms. Fambry, telling me that fighting was absolutely forbidden and she was surprised at me.

I tried to tell her what happened, the unjust act that triggered the whole thing. She kept repeating that I was fighting and that I would not be able to play if I did it again.

I noticed that Dylan was not in the time-out corner. He was over playing on the climbing bars, laughing.

This is when I made a mental note to myself. Life was unfair. And I'd better learn how to really fight someday so I could knock the Dylans of the world on their own fat cans.

JOSH WAS A Dylan. I was not the same Michael.

I drove Romeo's hammer into McBurney's Point. That's

130

the spot just above the belt line on the right side of the human body. Normally it's where a doctor might poke you to find out if you have pain associated with appendicitis.

I was giving Josh the pain associated with my fist.

He doubled over and dropped to his knees.

The white football player made his first, and last, aggressive move. With my left foot I made his right knee bend the other way. Down he went.

The black guy's face was a riot of conflicting emotions. He did not want to back away and lose face. But his two buddies were on the ground in various states of moan. It was now just him and me.

I motioned him forward with my index finger.

He just stood there, his fists raised to stomach level.

The mother of the boy who'd been splashed was hugging him and also looking at me. Her face reflected a certain horror at what she'd seen. She was afraid of me, afraid of what her child had just witnessed.

I couldn't blame her.

"Would you mind calling the police?" I said.

The black guy was now attending to his fallen counterpart. Josh was trying to get his breath back.

Another black gentleman, about sixty years old and wearing a newsboy-type hat, came over. He was smiling. "I saw the whole thing," he said. "You did right."

"Thanks," I said. "I have an appointment. Would you mind telling the police what you saw?"

"I'll tell 'em exactly what happened," he said. "What's your name, son?"

"Just tell them it was a guy who used to live around here," I said.

Then I walked around the corner and got in my car.

No one tried to stop me.

THE CAMPUS OF the University of California at Los Angeles is in the heart of a place called Westwood. It's a pretty campus, full of that old college look. Brick buildings of European design right next to modern classrooms. I walked along a path that was a nerve center of activity, students going every which way, backpacks slung and heads down over phones, and tables with various clubs passing out literature.

As I passed one called *Green Bliss,* a blonde of sunny disposition called to me and asked if I'd like to see a documentary playing on campus that night.

"What's it about?" I said.

"Ecology, economy, and equity," she said.

"Exceedingly, exponentially excellent," I said.

She smiled. "What's it say on your arm?"

"Vincit Omnia Veritas."

"Is that your name?"

"It's Latin. It means truth conquers all things. Do you believe in truth?"

She frowned. "I believe in people."

"All people?"

"Sure."

"Even bad people?"

"Nobody's really all bad," she said.

"Hitler?"

"I don't know that much about him."

"Nazi dictator. Gassed millions of Jews?"

"Well ..."

"The Holocaust?"

"I've heard of that."

"Ever had a class on it?"

She shook her head. "I study peace."

"History is about war."

"War is not the answer."

"Never?"

132

"Never."

"Not even against Nazis?"

"I don't know that much about them."

I fought back a dark despair and said, "I'd love to stay and chat, but I have an appointment back in reality."

She cocked her head.

That seemed like a good place to leave it.

I FINALLY FOUND the Life Sciences Building and looked for Pasfield's office on the directory. I went up to the second floor where I was met by a receptionist. She looked like an ecology major. On the wall behind her were two posters. One of them was a white background with a giant handprint formed from a pattern of green trees. The other was a campaign poster for Allison Ursula Serret. In the poster she was smiling, palms up, holding a sun in one hand and a moon in the other.

I asked the receptionist if the professor was in and she said he had class for another hour, and if I'd like to come back.

I said I would. She asked me what it was about and I said it was about the rally at the beach.

The receptionist beamed. "Are you working for Allison?"

"No," I said. "But I do live at the beach."

"That must be nice."

"It is."

"As long as we can keep it."

"It's doing pretty well," I said.

She didn't know what to say to that. So I left.

I went to a food court and bought a Coke and some chili cheese fries. I hate waiting anywhere without a book, but I was bookless. There was a copy of the student newspaper, *The Daily Bruin*, sitting on the table next to me.

Beggars can't be choosers.

The front page had a story about students protesting a

proposed tuition hike. They were mad at the Board of Regents. The Board of Regents was mad at Sacramento, the state capital.

Everyone assumed that some form of government action was the answer.

I had to marvel at how no one learns the lessons of history.

So I turned to the sports section. UCLA was about to play its cross-town rival, USC, in football. This is a big deal every year. It gives the kiddies a chance to go tribal, swill beer, and pretend this all matters.

I turned to the editorial page, hoping to find some engaging and intelligent argumentation.

Finding none, I turned to the movie reviews. After reading several grammatical errors I tossed the paper aside and sat amid college life.

A life I'd experienced too young and that ended too quickly.

I finished my fries and Coke and went on a little walk around the campus. When I got back to Terasaki, the professor was in.

"WHAT CAN I do for you, Mr. Romeo?"

Dr. Gary Pasfield sat behind his desk but did not offer to shake my hand. Instead he adjusted a mini-greenhouse the size of a small fish tank. It had a blue LED light zapping nourishment to what looked like sprigs of parsley.

Find points of connection. Get him talking about what interests him. Standard interview technique.

I nodded at a framed photograph on his wall of a handsome lad with an oar. "One of your students?"

He followed my gaze. "My son. That was taken a few years ago, when he was rowing for Stanford at the Pac-12 Championships."

"He looks like he could really churn it."

"Oh yes," he said. "All-American."

"What's he doing now?"

"He works for Google."

I nodded. "Everyone will work for Google someday, right?"

Pasfield laughed. "Or Amazon. Now, Mr. Romeo, what can I help you with?"

"May I sit?"

"For a moment."

I took a seat and said, "What exactly is integrative ecology?"

"Well," he said, "the whole field of ecology has become increasingly interdisciplinary. Even the social sciences have something to say, and should. Not to mention biology and horticulture."

"You can lead a horticulture, but you can't make her think," I said.

He didn't smile.

"Dorothy Parker quote," I said. "What's your current research focused on?"

"Land surface temperatures, mostly," he said.

"Global warming?"

"Climate change. Can we get to it, Mr. Romeo? I have a faculty meeting in half an hour and have to prep. Is this about the county supervisor campaign?"

"No, sir, it's not. I was at the rally at the beach, though."

"What did you think?"

"Good street dogs."

"Excuse me?"

"A vendor there. Don't you think street dogs should be legal?"

He took an annoyed breath. "Why are you here?"

I said, "I'm an investigator. I'm looking into a missing persons case."

"And what's that got to do with me?"

"Have you ever been to a place called Kahuna's?"

He frowned. "Isn't that a place down by the beach?"

"Right, Malibu."

"I think it's popular with the students. Some kind of margarita night or something."

"That's the place."

"I don't think I've been there," he said. "Or if I did, it was when we first moved out here."

"Your family?"

"My wife, son, and I."

"When was that?"

"Ten years ago. I came from the University of North Carolina. We love it out here. Except for the occasional earthquake. But you learn something when that happens. The earth does it to us every now and then, just to remind us who's boss."

"The earth is boss?"

"Don't you think so?"

"I think of it more as a giant beach house."

He thought about it, but the thought did not manifest itself in a verbal response.

"I do want to leave the beach house clean and neat," I said. "But it doesn't own me."

"Would you mind telling me why you're here?"

"There's a guy who works Kahuna's, big guy, bartender. I had a casual conversation with him yesterday. We exchanged pleasantries. He happened to have your card on him so I was curious if you knew this fellow."

"Is there a reason you're asking me other than curiosity?"

"Curiosity has to be part of what I do. I don't have much to go on right now, and I'm just gathering as much information as possible. The inductive method, if you will."

"You say he's a very big man?"

"You wouldn't forget him."

He looked up. "Let me think."

"Take your time," I said.

He did. Then, "I'm sorry, but I'm not getting anything."

"You sure?"

"If it's not coming, it's not coming. I really wish I could help you."

"Maybe you still can," I said.

He looked at me and waited.

I said, "Have you heard of any movement or sect that has the archangel Michael as a focus?"

"Archangel Michael? Like from the Bible?"

"That'd be the one."

He shook his head.

I took the picture of Brooklyn out of my wallet and handed it to Pasfield.

"Who is she?" he said.

"Her name is Brooklyn Christie."

"Is she a student?"

"No."

"Then I'm allowed to say she's pretty."

"Good old First Amendment," I said. "Even at UCLA."

"Sometimes," he said with a sideways smile. He handed the picture back to me. "I don't know who she is."

I stood. "Maybe your son can find her."

He looked confused.

"He works for Google, after all," I said.

"Ah," Pasfield said.

The man could grow parsley, but what he needed was a sense of humor.

AS I WAS rolling back to the beach, my phone bleeped.

"Mike, it's Rodney."

"What's up?"

"You said to tell you if he came back. The guy with the tattoo down the arm."

"He's there?"

"Just now. He walked in. No car."

"Is he on the beach?"

"Yeah. I can see him. Know what? I think he wants me to see him. I think he wants you to know he's here."

"Good instincts, Rodney. I'll park at my place then head up the cliffs the back way."

"Sure thing, Mike."

The Cove has lowlands and highlands. To get to the high ground you can go through the gate arm that Rodney controls. Or you can go around the back of the park, the long way. My mobile unit is a few spaces up from the gate, so I never have to drive through. I pulled into my driveway, popped the trunk, and got a pair of binoculars.

Then I jogged the back way and up the hill. It was a good workout. Spartacus was helping me stay in shape. What a guy.

I got to the top where I had an unobstructed view of the beach. I chose a spot where there was some native scrub and peered through it, like a spy in a World War II movie.

Spartacus was down there, alone, which was odd. He didn't seem to me to be the kind of guy that didn't have retinue. He had on black swim trunks. He was stretching, letting a couple of young ladies nearby get a load of his pecs.

I watched him for about ten minutes. He did a little walking around. Every now and then he'd look towards the parking lot like he expected somebody—me, for instance—to show up.

And then he'd glance up at the bluffs.

Where I was.

Now why would he do that?

I started a scan of the hillside below me.

Not a thing. A few clumps of native California plant life were big enough hide a—

Something glinted in the sun.

It was just for a second but as noticeable as a diamond. And it was coming from the clumps.

I made a visual impression of the location, then walked further down the road. I peered over the shoulder again.

No sign of anyone.

I waited, looked at Spartacus again, then back at the clumps.

Something moved. Something metallic.

It shifted position in someone's hands.

It was, in fact, a rifle.

Were they kidding?

I gathered up five rocks, a little smaller than a baseball and a little larger than a walnut. I tossed one at the clump.

The clump answered with a verbal WTF bomb.

I chucked another one, this time with a little heat on it. I heard it thump, then heard a wailing and a shower of curses bursting from the native foliage.

Trying not to laugh, I went back to my car and drove a little further down, until I could see the dirt parking lot that serves this side of the hill. It wasn't long before a guy carrying a duffel bag spilled into the lot. I recognized him as one of the guys I'd encountered along with Sparty that day at the beach.

He got to a silver BMW, opened the trunk, threw the duffel in, slammed the trunk. He got in and spun dirt as he pulled away. I wasn't able to see his plates. He emerged back at the flatland lot and drove out. Rodney waved at him.

I took another look at the beach. Sparty was talking to a girl. Then he took a phone out of his trunks and put it to his ear. Half a minute later he shoved it back in his trunks and went running toward the gate, then up the road toward PCH. Where rifle guy was probably waiting for him.

So Spartacus had come to see me.

I thought it was about time I went to see him.

WHICH IS WHY I went back to Ira's.

On the way I called Sophie. I wanted to tell her about my, um, conversation with Josh. But it went to voicemail and I left a message. I gave her the number for my untraceable phone, which was a risk, but one I was willing to take. I tried to sound charming, ended up like a bad comedian on open-mike night.

As soon as I entered the living room, which doubles as Ira's office, he read my face like the former cryptographer he is.

"Business or personal?" he said.

"What?"

"Your concerns."

"Universal," I said. "I'm worried about the cosmos."

"My advice is that you specialize," Ira said. "How about some tea?"

"Again with the tea?"

"Ah, yes. Coffee?"

"If it won't disrupt your sensibilities to make some."

"I've been adjusting my sensibilities ever since you arrived in Los Angeles, Michael. Make yourself at home." He started to wheel himself toward the kitchen, paused. "This is your home, you know."

He gave me the Ira Rosen smile which is a mix of wisdom, charm, and puckishness.

I scanned one of Ira's bookshelves. A volume called *Good and Evil in Jewish Thought* seemed like light reading. I carried it over to a wingback chair by the window and opened it up.

I was into a section on the dual nature of man when Ira came back with a tray on his lap.

"What are you reading?" he said.

"What the rabbis say about good and evil."

He handed me a cup of coffee from the tray. "And where do we come out on the issue?"

"You're for good and against evil."

"Whew," said Ira. "I was worried there for a moment."

"And that man is messed up without the restraint of a moral law," I said.

"All you have to do is watch the news," Ira said. "There is nothing new under the sun, my boy."

"Also, somebody wants to kill me."

Ira arched his snowy eyebrows.

I said, "A guy with a rifle wanted to pick me off at the Cove today."

"That's not good."

"Thank you," I said.

"I mean for the Cove," Ira said. "I wanted you there so as not to attract more trouble."

"Your concern overwhelms me."

"You can take care of yourself. But there are families there."

"So what now?" I said. "Shall I become a wanderer in the earth?"

"That would put the earth at risk," Ira said. "No, best that you stay here where I can keep an eye on you. Now why would someone want to shoot you, Michael? Is this related to the Christie matter?"

I shook my head. "I have another client."

"Why don't I know about this?"

"It's *pro bono*. I'm helping him find his guitar."

Ira went into one of his stone-cold silences that demands you fill the void.

"Remember that guy I told you about?" I said. "Had a little run-in at the beach?"

"He was swearing around children," Ira said.

"That's the one. He stole a guitar from the kid who calls himself C Dog."

"Carter," Ira said. "A rather laid-back young lad."

"Loves his music," I said.

"And his marijuana," Ira said.

"What happened is this guy, who I call Spartacus because of his tat, stole the guitar to bait me. At least I think he did. Maybe he's just mean."

"No restraint of moral law," Ira said.

"So he shows up at the Cove. I got a tip from Rodney. I went up on the bluffs and watched him. That's when I spotted the shooter. I rooted him out with some rocks."

"Rocks?"

"The Scottish way," I said. "He packed his gun and took off."

"Your life becomes exceedingly complex," Ira said.

"Some of us have that gift," I said. "The Spartacus tattoo is distinctive. Maybe we can search for a similar image, find him or the artist."

"A fishing expedition, eh?"

"Better than a needle in a haystack."

"Piffle," Ira said. "Give me something hard."

"All right," I said. "Where did Cain get his wife?"

"Cain was able," Ira said.

We repaired to Ira's computer station. It took him less than five seconds to bring up a page of images related to gladiator tattoos.

He scrolled through the thumbnails slowly, so I could look on. There were some pretty impressive inks. Helmeted warriors, armor, shields, bows. Even a coliseum scene.

And then about halfway down, a guy showing off the exact tattoo I'd seen. You could only see the lower half of his face, but in the background were all sorts of framed art pieces, the unmistakable décor of a tattoo shop.

"That's got to be it," I said.

Ira clicked on the image. The sidebar identified it as Bat's Ink Eclectic. It was on Melrose in Hollywood.

"Voilà," Ira said.

"Next time, make it faster," I said.

I CALLED RAY Christie and set up a meeting for the next day.

Sophie had not called me back.

Sometimes things in this life bother you without your consent. The Stoics would have argued that point, but I think the Stoics had a stick up their togas. The human mind, as well-oiled as some can make it, is still subject to the slings and arrows of the flesh.

Pascal said the heart has its reasons which reason knows nothing of. He was talking about faith in God there, but he might just as well have been talking about love.

Ira challenged me to a game of chess, and that seemed like just the ticket. Ira got the white pieces and chose to open with his Queen's pawn. I came at him with the Cambridge Springs Defense, a favorite of Dr. Emanuel Lasker. He's something of a hero of mine. A doctorate in mathematics and a writer of philosophical speculations, he also happened to be chess champion of the world for twenty-seven years.

His most effective move, they say, was to blow a plume of cigar smoke at an opponent who was deep in thought.

My kind of guy.

The game with Ira lasted two-and-a-half hours and went to thirty-four moves. When I got his King and Rook in a vicious Knight fork, he resigned.

"Bravo," he said.

"Still got it," I said.

"I shall take it from you next time."

"Look forward to it."

That night I dreamed of chess. I was playing against the devil. He was smoking a cigar. I said, "If you blow smoke at me I'll pull your horns off."

"Go ahead and try," the devil said.

That's when the dream ended.

THE NEXT MORNING I drove out to the Valley to meet with Ray Christie. On the way, the news reported that a massive fire had broken out downtown in the early morning hours, taking out a huge apartment tower that was under construction, damaging two other buildings and leaving freeways and roads closed.

Officials suspected arson.

The developer of the project vowed to rebuild.

And I thought about the nut with that published diatribe, the one who claimed to have exploded the development near the Getty.

I MET RAY Christie at a little café called Aroma in Studio City. He said he'd found it driving around one night when he couldn't sleep. It's a coffee place with a hipster veneer. Maybe that helped him feel closer to his daughter.

He bought me a coffee and we sat outside at a back table.

I gave him what I had, leaving out the parts where somebody tried to kill me. I figured he was dealing with enough stress. He certainly looked like it. There were bags under his eyes and his hands shook a little.

"Do you think the police will ever find her?" he said, in a tone that sounded like he meant her corpse.

Of course that's a question I couldn't answer. But it was a

desperate father's plea. "If they and I are both working on it, we'll be operating on all cylinders."

"Don't they say that if you don't find somebody in the first forty-eight hours they're probably dead?"

"I think that's only for children."

"She's my child," he said.

That got to me.

I said, "How many times did you talk to your daughter before you came out here?"

"Only twice. On the phone."

"Was there anything that she said that might lead you to believe she was hiding anything?"

"Like what?"

"A person. Somebody she might've been involved with, or afraid of. Afraid to talk to you about it?"

He thought about it a moment and shook his head. "No, she was only upbeat. Like she had found some new thing to get involved in. She was always getting involved in things when she was little. She'd go crazy about something for a while, then drop it for something else. It was all in for her. She never did anything halfway."

"Does the name Lindsay mean anything to you?"

He thought about it, looking down at the table. "Yes, it does. Lindsay. A friend of Brooklyn's. When she first came out here she told me she was going to stay with her."

"Do you have a last name?"

"Yeah, yeah … DeSalvo. That was it. I remembered it because of the Boston Strangler."

"Albert DeSalvo," I said.

"Yeah. I remember thinking that's a real unfortunate name to have."

"Did she give you an address, a phone number?"

He shook his head and took a sip of coffee. He had to hold the coffee cup with both hands.

"Maybe you ought to check with a doctor," I said.

"It's just lack of sleep," he said. "They say some of your best ideas can come when you tired."

"Your body needs rest, Mr. Christie."

"Do you have somebody close to you, Mr. Romeo? A daughter or a wife or girlfriend?"

"Right now it's a friend. He's a rabbi."

"I'm not a religious man, but sometimes I wish I was."

"I think that's the same for a lot of people."

AFTER THE MEETING with Ray Christie I drove Spinoza to Bat's Ink Eclectic on Melrose. The front door led to a set of stairs. At the foot of the stairs was a print of a tattooed lady from old carnival days. A dialogue bubble over her head said, "You must be 18 years of age or older to go upstairs, Cutie Pie."

I figured I qualified on both counts and went up.

The wood-and-glass doors opened into a nicely appointed reception area. This was clearly no kiosk at the waterfront with an old salt named Dusty ready to mark your forearm with Mom. This was high-class presented to upscale customers.

A young woman with black hair, black leotard, and a set of sleeves down to her wrists and halfway onto the back of her hands, looked up from a desk and greeted me with a smile.

"Welcome to Bat's," she said.

"Thanks."

"Do you have an appointment?"

"No. I was hoping I could talk to the proprietor. Would that be Bat?"

She nodded. "He's with someone right now. Would you like to wait?"

"I would."

"What were you interested in getting? Or would you like to see some ideas?"

"I'll dream some up."

"That's cool. Can I see your arm?"

I showed her.

"That's Latin, isn't it?" she said.

"It's nice to know someone still recognizes the language," I said.

"What's it mean?"

"It either means truth conquers all things, or make mine pastrami on rye."

She frowned, then laughed. "That's funny. Or not."

"Not?"

"Wee don't like to think about bad translations on somebody's skin, you know?"

"Ah," I said.

"Like when Britney got that Chinese symbol on her hip."

"Britney?"

"Spears."

"I remember her."

"It was supposed to be Chinese for *mysterious*. But it actually meant *strange*. Then she got Hebrew script for God, but it was misspelled."

"Bummer," I said.

"And David Beckham had his wife's name inked on his arm in Sanskrit. And misspelled her name."

"Sanskrit's a tricky language."

"Tell me about it," she said. Then she paused, her eyes doing a quick scan of the canvas that was my body.

"You with anybody?" she said.

"Nope, came alone."

"I mean, *with*. Like in your personal life."

"Are you putting a move on me?" I said.

"Uh-huh," she said.

"You don't know anything about me."

"That's what the move is for."

She smiled.

"I'm flattered," I said.

"You should be. I'm very picky."

"But in the interest of full disclosure, I am with someone."

"Is it serious?"

"It might be."

"Then you're still on the market!"

My mouth was dry.

"See," she said, "way I think about it, you don't close off all your options just because you've got one over here that might work out." She put her arm out to the side and opened her hand, like she was one half of a scale. "What you do"—she put her other hand out now and made a juggling motion—"is play around, try things, you know?"

"Boy, you make it tough."

"Then surrender."

"I feel like The Alamo."

"The what?"

"The little mission where a small group of Americans were confronted by thousands of Mexican troops."

"I don't know about that."

"It happened a long time ago. They were asked to surrender, and refused."

"What happened?"

"They all died."

"There you go!" she said. "You don't want to die, to you?"

I laughed. It felt good to laugh. "You're going to go a long way in this world. I must regretfully refuse. But I want to thank you for asking."

"I tried," she said. "Why don't you have a seat and think about it?"

"Always good to think," I said, and quickly sought a chair.

TEN MINUTES LATER a woman came into the reception room with a smile. With her was a short, bald man with tat sleeves of crowded complexity. The man consulted with the flirtatious receptionist and the woman plopped her purse on the desk.

Then the man turned to me and stuck out his hand. "I'm Bat."

"Phil."

"I got the colors if you got the time."

We shook hands.

"What's on your arm?" he asked.

I showed him.

"What's that? Some kind of name?"

"It's a Latin."

"Right on," he said. "How 'bout something above and below?"

"I'm not here to get inked," I said.

"No? Then what are you here for?"

"To date me," the receptionist said.

Bat looked at her and back at me. "Watch out for her."

"Maybe we can talk in your studio," I said.

He took me there. It was large room with a hardwood floor and two ornate tattoo chairs in the middle. With a couple of décor changes it could have been an old-school barber shop.

"You sure you're not in the market?" Bat said. "Because you are a fresh canvas that is just crying out for art."

"I'm trying to track down someone," I said. "I think you might know who it is."

"Track down? That doesn't sound good."

"I work for a lawyer."

"That never sounds good," he said.

"You have a point," I said. "But it's important. It involves a valuable piece of property I'm trying to recover for the owner. I believe this fellow I'm looking for may be a crucial link—or maybe I should say, a crucial ink—in this chain."

Bat smiled. "I like you, Phil. But what have I got to do with it?"

"The guy I'm looking for has a sort of gladiator tat, covers his chest here, shoulder, then goes down his arm. Black ink, looks like chain mail."

"Yeah, that's my work all right. I know exactly who you're talking about."

"Great."

He said nothing.

"Let's start with his name," I said.

"No can do," Bat said. "You know, all that's confidential."

"It doesn't have to be," I said.

"Just the way I do business."

"Your business is making money, right?"

"And customer loyalty."

I nodded. "And this guy is someone you feel loyalty to?"

At that he didn't say anything, either. But he frowned a little.

"What is it?" I said.

"Well ..."

"Go ahead."

"It's just that this guy's an ..." He paused for a second, then finished with a common urban vernacular for an undesirable.

"Then maybe loyalty isn't all it's cracked up to be," I said. "Loyalty is owed where loyalty is earned."

"Maybe."

"Would a little financial incentive help?" I said.

"I've looked a lot of people in the face," Bat said. "In my line that's what you do. You get so you can tell things."

I nodded. "You can observe a lot just by watching, as Yogi Berra would say."

"Hey, you know about Yogi Berra?"

"My grandfather was a Yankee fan," I said.

"Cool! Mine, too."

"Serendipity," I said.

He got thoughtful again. "So yeah, faces. I'm gonna ask you something straight up, and you answer me straight up, okay?"

"You got a deal."

"If I give you this name, you gonna do harm to this guy?"

"That is not my intent or purpose," I said. "All I want is to retrieve a valuable item from him."

"What if he doesn't give it to you?"

"I will let the law handle that," I said. What I meant was that I'd crack some ribs and loosen some teeth, and if Spartacus wanted to sue me, I'd let him. But I didn't explain any further.

"That's good enough for me," Bat said. "So what were you thinking this info is worth?"

"How about a C note?"

"Two is what I was thinking," he said.

"You going to dicker with me? For a simple lookup?"

He put his hands out. "Business."

The strongest negotiating position you can have is the ability to walk away. The second strongest is to make the other guy *think* you're going to walk away. The third strongest is the ability to read what kind of guy the other guy is.

I said, "See you," and turned to go.

"Whoa," Bat said. "Okay, one-fifty."

I turned.

"So I can take my wife out to a nice dinner," he said.

Fishing for the bills I said, "I'm all for good marriages."

Bat took the money and went to a back office for a couple of minutes. I looked at the art work on the walls. He came back and gave me a slip of paper. It had a name, Rocky Boada, and an address in Reseda.

FROM BAT'S PALACE of fine art I walked to a café with some outside tables. I sat at one that gave me a view of squat palm trees, store awnings, and pink and blue and red buildings shoulder to shoulder. And one billboard advertising the annual let-Meryl-Streep-win-another-Oscar movie.

A waitress dressed like a beat poet from 1959 came unsmilingly to my table and handed me a menu and asked what I'd like to drink.

"I think I'll go wild and order a beer," I said.

Unsmilingly, she said, "What kind of beer would you like?"

"Alcoholic," I said.

"I mean, we have a Scottish ale with a roasted pumpkin spice note, an Oktoberfest with Bavarian Hops, an IPA with citrus zest flavors—"

"Schlitz," I said. "Do you have Schlitz?"

"I don't think so. What is that?"

"Never mind," I said. "How about you choose one for me? Bring me one with the most zest and the least pumpkin."

She looked at me, yes, without a smile and tried to process the request. "Okay. I think."

"And some kind of cheeseburger."

"Do you prefer cheddar, Swiss, feta, goat—?"

"Wait a second," I said. I closed my eyes and touched the menu randomly with my index finger. I looked at the result.

"I'll have the Parisian fromage bleu. I guess."

"And how would you like that cooked?"

"With a touch of sunset pink in the middle."

She looked at me. She didn't smile.

"You're joking with me," she said.

"Medium would be fine," I said.

Then I used my phone to do a little research on Lindsay DeSalvo.

Got her Facebook and Twitter accounts, and a reference on IMDB, the movie database.

IMDB had some pictures of her. Her best photo showed a pretty face with auburn hair and eyes with a hint of animal-at-play in them. Like a pre-Tom Cruise Nicole Kidman.

According to the credits she'd been in a few movies, none of which I'd heard of. They looked like indie slasher types. She had one TV credit as "Waitress" on *Two and a Half Men*.

But at the top there was a project called *Dead Man's Hand* that was listed as being in pre-production. I clicked to the listing page and saw this squib: *An alien from space lands in the Dakota Territory in 1875, tracking the time-traveling killer of his brother.*

I took a look at the cast and didn't see any names I was familiar with.

Except one.

The actor set to play Wild Bill Hickok was none other than Jon-Scott Morrow.

Listed two places under him, billed as "Sally," was Lindsay DeSalvo.

Connecting wires started snapping in the back of my neck, looking for a full charge.

CHOMPING MY PARISIAN fromage bleu burger and sipping an ale that was affable without being chummy, I used Google Earth to scope out the neighborhood where Rocky "Spartacus" Boada lived. Reseda was one of the booming L.A. suburbs sixty years ago, when aerospace was taking off and returning GIs were having kids right and left. It's dropped in status since the space race wheezed to a close and businesses were chased out because California's spend-like-a-drunk and tax-like-a-king ways worked their inevitable economic consequences.

After my fine dining, I drove there.

And cruised by the address.

It was a single-family home, gray with white trim. Probably built in 1960. Two-car garage. And on the side of the garage a wall-unit air conditioner sticking its butt out the window.

I made a U-turn at the corner and came back the other way. I paused just past the garage and could hear the air conditioner humming.

On a cool day in the Valley.

There was also a security camera directed at the side of the garage.

One could surmise that there was some growing going on in that garage. Hippie lettuce. And much more than the six plants the new California laws allowed for. The air conditioner was to keep things cool because of the heat generated by grow lights.

It was a good working theory.

One other item of note. The silver BMW in the driveway, looking very much like the one used by the would-be shooter at the Cove.

I PARKED A few houses down and across the street.

Joey Feint used to say, "Ninety percent of surveillance is waiting. Five percent is coffee. The other five percent is knowing where to pee."

He was a poet, that Joey.

Lacking coffee, I wasn't too worried about that last five percent. But it did give me time to think out loud.

Brooklyn Christie had been missing for at least two weeks. When she talked to her father she seemed agitated about something, hyped up about finding "the way of life."

That would be exciting all right. We've been looking for it for six thousand years.

In the brief time I'd known Brooklyn Christie, she struck me as someone highly vulnerable, even suggestible. She was like the Amaryllis—blooming with vibrant color but fading fast if not given the right soil. Such flowers are prone to getting picked.

The phrase "way of life" sounded pseudo-spiritual. Which suggested anything from Scientology to a start-up guru. Could have been a megachurch, of which L.A. has many. Or even a multi-level marketing scheme.

That little bit of information from Brooklyn wasn't going to get me anywhere. She could have been on a retreat. Wasn't there some guy you had pay big bucks in order to fly to an island and bask in his effluvia for a week or two? Which people actually did? Lots of people?

Brooklyn might have been ripe for just such a plucking.

But it was a shot in the dark.

And was her disappearance—or not wishing to communicate—connected to her condition on the beach that day? Maybe, or the two could have been totally unrelated and random. Like so many things that make life into life and not the outline for a perfectly plotted script.

What was more promising was the triangle made up of Lindsay DeSalvo, Jon-Scott Morrow, and Brooklyn.

Lindsay had a role in an upcoming Western starring Jon-Scott Morrow.

Lindsay was Brooklyn's friend.

Making it likely that the house Brooklyn had stumbled out of, poisoned, was that of Wild Bill Hickok.

I'd have to ride my horse on over there again and give the aging lawman another chance to talk.

A bright-red Corvette convertible passed me. The kid at the wheel looked about fifteen. He wore shades and a black cap, backwards, white kid gangsta style. He was probably a product of the L.A. Unified School system.

And the 'Vette was probably a present from mommy and daddy.

Or maybe he was a rock star.

Either way, he pulled up in front of Rocky's house and got out.

THROUGH BINOCULARS I watched the kid, whose stick legs stuck out of long black flop shorts that went to mid calf, walk up to the door and knock. He looked up once and made a quasi-gang sign. Either that or his hand cramped. There was obviously a camera looking down at him.

Then the door opened and there was Spartacus, in white T and black jeans and bare feet.

He gave the kid some slap-doodled handshake. They jawed, then the kid went inside.

Door closed.

Two minutes later, door opened.

Kid came walking out fast, his thug pants flapping in the breeze.

I started my car and drove by, noting a bulge in his right pocket as he got into his Corvette.

Half a block down, I parked at the curb and got out.

The hot red car was making its way down the street at a good clip.

I started to walk across the street.

Tire squeal.

The kid leaned on the horn.

I put my hands up as if to say *sorry*.

And hit my chest as if to say *my bad*.

He honked again.

I jumped up on the hood.

Then over the windshield.

A little twist and I was in the passenger seat.

"Whoa whoa whoa!" the kid said.

His phone was sitting in a cup holder on the console. I grabbed it.

"Whoa!"

"Ease over to the curb," I said.

"What're you doin', man?"

"You want your phone back?'

"Yeah!"

"You want to live?"

His chin went down a floor.

"Do you want these nice wheels not to go up in flames?"

A quavering voice said, "Don't kill me, man. Take my money."

"I don't want your money," I said. "And I don't want to smell your fear. You're going to do one thing for me, and then I'm going to let you go, never to see you again."

The small body of the white gangster-in-training shook like a horse's leg trying to get rid of a fly.

FIVE MINUTES LATER the kid stood at Rocky's front door. He was still shaking. But he knew the deal. It had taken me one full minute to explain it to him, about thirty seconds for his questions, another thirty for clarification, and a minute to calm him down and keep him from crying.

Now as I stood just off the doorway, out of reach of the camera, I held in my left fist a roll of quarters that I keep in Spinoza's glove compartment for such times as this. In my right I held the kid's phone.

I nodded at the kid.

He knocked on the door.

A couple of seconds of silence, then the door whipped open.

"Whattaya want?" Rocky said. "Don't you keep coming—"

That was all he was able to mouth. I whipped around and

plowed my reinforced left fist straight into the ersatz gladiator's snout.

He dropped like a bag of cement.

"Here," I said, handing the trembling guy his phone. He snatched it and ran away.

I stepped over Rocky's inert body.

The inside was strewn with items and a man mess of open pizza boxes, beer bottles, a table with white powder on it, and a wall-size TV that was on mute but had some pornographic movie in mid-scene.

And there in a corner, pretty as you please, was C Dog's guitar.

Moving fast, I went for it, then saw something move on my right.

He was in boxers, that was all. I recognized him immediately.

Rifle Boy. My would-be assassin.

His eyes got pie size.

He turned and moved back from whence he came.

I knew he was going for a weapon.

Which made my adrenaline-laced pursuit all the quicker.

It was a bedroom.

Rifle Boy was leaning over a table, reaching for something. He was just turning with a nine-mil in his hand when I gave his face the left fist treatment.

He crumpled over the table, knocking a lamp to the floor.

That's when I heard the first scream.

IN IRISH FOLKLORE, the Banshee is a spirit, in the form of a woman, who wails with a chilling screech outside a home where someone is about to die. The Banshee's wail chills the blood and pierces the heart.

My blood went into the freezer.

Another scream, and from the bed a girl came at me. She wasn't dressed in rags, nor was she gray of hair and red of eyes like that Celtic spook. She was young. My mind triggered the thought *fifteen or sixteen years old.* She wore a Philadelphia Eagles T-shirt and black panties.

She did have claws. They were outstretched as she jumped me.

My cage instincts were in working order. I leaned back as the first swipe of her nails scratched air.

Her screams melted into obscenities even a Banshee would find over-the-top.

Then she came at me again, arms wild, and I was sure she was high. Her tangle of nut-brown hair fumed like sea spray as she shook her head wildly. I got hold of her wrist and gave her a takedown. It didn't take much. She must have weighed all of a hundred pounds.

"You killed him!" she said, the first rational expression of the encounter.

"He's not dead," I said.

She told me what I could do to myself.

"Be quiet," I said, bending her wrist a little more.

She yelped.

"Do what I say and you won't get hurt," I said.

She told me another thing I could do to myself.

Then I heard a moaning from the front room.

"Come along," I said as I lifted her and controlled her out to where I'd laid Rocky on the floor.

He was groaning and moving.

"Rocky!" the girl shouted. "Get up!"

Rocky shook his head.

I held the girl's arm with my right hand.

Rocky started to rise.

With my left fist of quarters, I put him to sleep again.

The girl gasped. Then started crying.

A voice from the bedroom cursed.

So I controlled her back to the bedroom, just as Rifle Boy was getting up.

I put him to sleep, too.

I was beginning to feel like one of those guys with the spinning plates, having to go back and froth, back and forth.

The girl found her voice again and screamed.

Time. For this, I did not have it.

I lifted the sputtering sprite into the air and threw her down on top of the bed sheet.

WITHIN FIVE SECONDS I had her wrapped up in the sheet like a Christmas present ... if the present was a live puma. I tied the corners like a Viking testing his strength after too much grog. Then I lifted the whole thing and put it in the closet and shut the door.

I went back to the living room, retrieved C Dog's guitar, and walked out of the house, closing the door gently behind me.

Down the block to my car. I put C's guitar in the trunk, then took out my phone and punched 911.

A dispatcher answered and I said, "Listen carefully." I gave her the address of Rocky's house, speaking slowly. Then added, "There is an underage girl who has been sexually molested and is tied up and in a closet. There are two men, bloody, with illegal weapons. So have guns drawn."

"Sir, I need a name and phone. Your number is not—"

"You have to move fast. Be sure to search the trunk of the BMW. Got that? And the garage. An illegal marijuana grow. Got that?"

"Yes, sir. But if you'll please give me your—"

"Sexually abused teenager," I said. "Hurry."

And clicked off.

I drove to the next big street, Vanowen, and parked. Looked at the time.

Three minutes elapsed until I heard the first siren.

I saw the flashing lights ten seconds later. The black-and-white passed me and hung a left.

Two minutes later, another screaming cop car roared by. My work here was done.

I headed back to the beach.

I WENT TO see C Dog.

I let myself in through his front screen door.

He was not expecting me. At least that's what I got from as his expression exploded into the look of the nabbed druggie. Next to him on a beanbag chair was a guy trying hard to look swarthy and bad. Your average thug works on his appearance as diligently as a prom queen. Since most of their act is about seeking respect, they have to put on a mask of practiced menace.

Such people bore the snot out of me. Try talking to them about anything but women and football and see how far you get.

One more thing. Sitting on a small table, on some tin foil, was a glass pipe and a lighter. The glass pipe was cloudy. The room had a faint, burned plastic odor.

"Hey man!" C Dog said with a big grin.

"Having a party, C?" I said.

"Who is this guy?" the bad man said. He wore jeans and an Oakland Raiders jersey.

"This's my bud," C Dog said. "Name's Mike. Mike, this is Chas."

"'Sup," Chas said.

"You bring the meth?" I said.

"Want some?"

C Dog started laughing. But I had the distinct feeling he didn't know what he was laughing at.

"I've got your guitar," I said.

C sat up like he'd been stung. "No way! Where is it?"

"You broke our agreement," I said.

His face went blank. "You gotta be kiddin' me, man. You got my guitar and you won't give it to me?"

"That's right. Agreements are conditional. You have not fulfilled your condition. You have broken your word."

"But it's my property!"

"No, it's my property. Collateral on our agreement."

"Give the man his ax, man," Chas said.

"You are not a party to the agreement," I said. "Why don't you go outside for a while and talk to the sky?"

"I don't gotta do nothin'."

"Maybe I should talk to him alone," C Dog said to Chas.

"You gonna take this in your own house, man?"

"And another thing," I said. "You don't bring any more of your product over here. Not for sale, not for using. That clear?"

The dealer's face flushed. He struggled to his feet out of the bean bag. He was a pretty big guy. He tried to look like a guy who'd been in a lot of fights.

Next thing I knew, the guy pulled a knife. A switchblade.

Flick.

Six-inch blade.

"Really?" I said.

"Put that away, man," C Dog said.

"Guy's not gonna to talk to me that way," Chas said. "Guy's gonna take off."

"Put the knife away, son," I said.

"You go get the man's guitar and come back with it," he said. "All you're gonna do tonight."

"I'm going to give you the chance to put the knife away

and walk out of here. You don't and I'm going to take it away from you and carve a large letter A on your left butt cheek. Did you ever read *The Scarlet Letter?* Let me answer that for you. No."

He frowned as if my English was his third language.

"Well, this A in your left butt cheek will not be for adultery. It is the first letter of what you are."

"Put the stick away, man," C Dog said.

"Nah," Chas said. "I want him to try. Thinks he can, he's gonna get cut."

"Never take out a knife when you're high," I said.

"Come get it," Chas said.

"Don't, man!" C Dog said, but it was impossible to know who he was talking to.

I took a step toward Chas.

He pushed out with the knife, pulled it back.

"This is not going to end well," I said.

"This my house!" C Dog said.

"Shut up," Chas said.

"You don't tell a man to shut up in his own house," I said. "You agree, don't you, C?"

I wanted C Dog to keep talking, and Chas to keep reacting. The best timing against a guy with knife is when he gets distracted, even a little. You watch his eyes and wait for the flinch.

"That's right!" C Dog said. "My house!"

Chas said. "Shut *up!*"

It was the *up* that did it. Chas put so much into it his whole body jerked.

I pounced.

He was holding the knife at gut level. I brought my right hand to his inner wrist and my left to the backside of his hand. This was simultaneous, like I was giving one big clap.

The move snaps the hand inward and the fingers open automatically.

The knife hit the floor.

Chas was too shocked for words. I put him in a hammer lock and forced him to the floor, face down.

I picked up the knife and straddled his back, facing his feet. I used the knife to slice the seat of his jeans.

"Hey, man!" C Dog said.

I put the knife down on the small of Chas's back and used my hands to rip open the jeans.

I picked up the knife and pressed the point into his left butt cheek.

Chas grunted into the floor.

"That's the spot where the A is gonna go," I said.

"Get off me!" Chas said.

I reversed my position so I was sitting facing his head. I leaned over and said, "You don't come back to the Cove, ever. You do, and I will carve that A on one cheek and the Gettysburg Address on the other. We clear?"

He bared his teeth but nothing came out.

"Tell me we're clear," I said. "Or I begin with *Fourscore and seven years ago.*"

"All right, man!" he said.

I got up, folded the knife and put it in my pocket.

"Get out," I said.

Chas the dealer got to his feet, gathering as much manhood as he had left—only enough to fill a thimble—and stormed out, jeans flapping.

I looked at C Dog. He had this awestruck look on his face.

He said, "You are one bad—"

"I don't want to hear another word out of you," I said. "We're done, you and me."

"Hey—"

I put up my hand. "Not. Another. Word. Unless you want what your friend got."

I pushed the screen door the rest of the way off and set it aside on the porch.

When I was about fifty feet away from C Dog's place, I heard his pitiful voice say, "But what about my guitar, man?"

THE NEXT DAY I went to see a man named Zane Donahue. He was the guy Jimmy Sarducci had set me up with. The guy who knew a guy who knew a guy ...

He lived in a house off San Vicente on the Westside. Gated driveway. When I drove up to the gate and pressed the buzzer, the gate opened and a woman who pumped iron and popped roids came out. No one looks this way naturally.

She wore a camouflage tank top and dark-blue bike pants. Her meaty thighs gave the Spandex a hearty stretch. Her arms were substantial and ripped. She wore her blonde hair in a pony tail. The expression on her face was a cross between an annoyed waitress and Chucky. But the meanest thing on her was a weapon. She wore it in a holster like a cop. It was bulky so I figured Taser.

Muscles approached my window. She waited for me to speak. If her face had not been laced with anabolics, it would have been pretty.

"I'm here to see Mr. Donahue," I said.

"Your name Romeo?" she said in a throaty voice that seemed itself to be lifting weights.

"Yes."

"ID?"

I showed her my very nice-looking fake driver's license I got some time ago from a street hustler. She shoved it back to me. Then opened the gate wide so I could drive in. I half expected Cerberus to be on a leash behind her.

There was a big circular driveway in front of a massive, English Tudor house. I parked Spinoza in front of the archway with a big wooden door and a thick knocker. I told myself not to repeat any lines from *Young Frankenstein* in front of the muscular gatekeeper, who came up and opened the door.

She used her thumb to invite me in.

I stepped into a spacious foyer. She told me to wait while patting her Taser. And off she went.

The foyer had marble floors and oak-paneled walls. On one side there was a Greek-style statue of a discus thrower. I liked that. Classic feel to all the money. On the other side was another sculpture, this one also in the Greek style. Two naked men in what looked like gladiatorial combat. Neither of them was Jewish.

Presently the muscled one returned and motioned for me to follow.

I was led past a living room the size of Union Station and a kitchen that could have hosted the Ice Capades. Through a window to my left I saw a large, kidney-shaped pool with an enclosed lanai and a barbecue pit a small family could live in.

We turned right and entered a room of red cedar, like a hunting lodge. A stone fireplace dominated one wall, and in the middle was a huge desk fashioned out of a slice of redwood tree trunk. It was free-form on the outside edges, horseshoe-shaped on the inside.

There were two computer monitors on the desk.

Behind one of the monitors, so I couldn't see his face, was a man who said, "Welcome, Mike Romeo."

"Thanks," I said.

"Be with you in a second. You want something to drink?"

"I'm good."

"Okay. Sid, you can go."

My escort made the now-familiar Taser pat and walked out.

I heard the clacking of keys and saw fingers moving under the monitor.

"Bam," he said as he finished off his symphony with one peck of his index finger. Then he stood and walked out from behind the desk to offer me his hand.

He was six feet tall, lean with a good grip. His hair was the color and thickness of steel wool. He wore a red golf shirt untucked over khaki trousers, and no shoes. His body seemed charged with electricity, lighting up his blue eyes from behind.

"I'm Zane," he said.

"Hi," I said.

"What do you think of the place?"

"Nice," I said.

"I'd say so! It was designed by Elmer Grey, same guy who did the Beverly Hills Hotel. You know who used to own this place?"

"Ringling Brothers?"

"Max Baer. Heavyweight champion of the world. You a fight fan?"

"A little."

"Max had a right, boy. He would've beat Joe Louis if he hadn't cracked his hand against Braddock."

"You're old school," I said.

"That's the *only* school. I want to bring it back. Honor. No fixes. And a gambler could make an honest buck."

It was hard to get a read on this man. He talked like he'd been born in 1920 and missed watching Friday Night Fights on a black-and-white TV set.

"Jimmy tells me you're one of his fighters."

"Jimmy exaggerates," I said.

"You look like a prospect. You'd do well to hook up with Jimmy. He knows the game."

"I'm not a fighter."

"Of course you are. We both know it. I can tell just by looking at you."

"You don't believe in that book and cover thing?"

"Not at all. I have judged many books by their covers. It's one of the reasons I am where I am today."

"And where is that exactly?" I said.

"So you see." He spread his arms wide. "This is only where I work. I own a house in Malibu and another in Rancho Santa Fe."

"We're practically neighbors," I said.

"I know."

"How do you know?"

"Information is the most valuable thing you can have in my business."

"I'm not sure what that business is."

"Let's go out by the pool," he said. "I insist you have a drink with me. What's your poison?"

"Lemonade."

"Bourbon it is."

HE PUT ON shades and we went out to his pool.

"It's the same shape as when Max owned it," he said. "I wanted to keep everything the way it was. As much as possible."

"Did the statues come with it?"

"In entrance hall? No, I commissioned those. I think we need to bring back that kind of art, don't you?"

"Old school again."

"Anything past 1960 should be outlawed."

We sat under the lanai and Donahue tapped something on his phone. Then: "See over there?"

He pointed across a large back lawn at some eucalyptus trees.

"On the other side is Riviera Country Club," he said. "I've watched Tiger, Phil, all the rest. What do you think of that?"

"I think you're very happy with it."

He frowned. "That's a strange answer."

"I've been accused of that."

"You had some information that you wanted. Is that right?"

"I would appreciate it," I said.

"I don't operate on an appreciation basis," Zane Donahue said. "I'm sure you can understand that."

"Businessman of sorts?"

"All business. We can work on a cash basis, or figure something else out."

"Let's try to figure something out."

The woman who'd opened the gate came out with a silver tray and a couple of drinks on it. Donahue and I took a glass and the woman returned to the house.

"I'm serious about you being a fighter," Donahue said. "I'd like to try you out."

"You're in the fight game?"

"I call it entertainment. You did some cage fighting once. I looked you up. There's not much else about you."

"I'm not that interesting," I said.

"Oh I don't think so," he said, smiling. "I don't think so at all. You have new identity written all over you."

Donahue took a sip of his drink. And I began to know two things about this guy. First, his power was legit, based on intelligence and insight. And second, behind the drinks and the smile was someone not to be messed with.

"Let me put it to you this way," he said. "I specialize in helping people who have, you know, questionable pasts. I can find employment for them, ways to make some good money. Ways to come back to life, so to speak. You might be one of those people I can help."

"Maybe I can help you," I said.

"And just how can you do that?"

"A little legal advice."

He laughed. "I got lawyers out my proverbial wazoo. Anything else?"

"Yes," I said. "Ancient wisdom."

"What are you talking about?"

"The wisdom of the Greeks."

"You are kidding me, right?"

"Not at all," I said. "And you like information. Greek wisdom is some of the most valuable information we can have in this life."

"And you are some kind of expert?"

"I've done a lot of reading, thinking about it."

"You fascinate me," he said. "Go ahead. Dazzle me with your brilliance."

I put my drink on the glass table between us, laced my fingers together and cracked my knuckles like a pianist. "One of the lessons of history is that powerful men fall because of hubris. It's a Greek idea that means outrageous arrogance. When the Persian Empire rose to prominence in the fifth and fourth centuries BC, it was an awesome thing. Eventually a king named Cyrus presided over a large and stable slice of Earth. But hubris overtook him. He tried to take over the land of the Scythians, what is modern day Afghanistan. He engaged in what we would call a preemptive war. It did not work. He overreached."

"Too bad for the Persians."

"In World War II, Hitler tried to take Stalingrad, not figuring on the fighting spirit of the Russian soldiers and the biggest kick in the butt, the Russian winter."

"Are you comparing me to Hitler?"

"I'm talking about hubris, which applies to everyone. Especially those with power. What I would suggest is that you fight that urge within you. Because power itself is not satisfying. There is never enough. You must find satisfaction in life elsewhere."

"You are the craziest person I've ever met, you know that? Who talks like this?"

"Now I've given you wisdom," I said, "maybe you can give me a name."

Zane Donahue smiled. "You've got some good attitude. How would you like to work for me?"

"I'm good where I am."

"Living like a bum at the beach?"

"Free from the encumbrances of wealth is how I put it."

Zane Donahue shook his head as if amused. "Money is a very nice thing to have."

"It's better than hives," I said, "but worse than content-ment."

"Man, you crack me up," he said. "What if I hired you to do some freelance work for me sometime?"

"I'm not hanging out a shingle or anything."

"Sure, sure. Just hypothetically. Would you consider it? I pay top dollar, and you must have expenses."

"I'll consider it," I said.

"Good." He slapped his thigh. "Now what is it you came to me about?"

"There's a bartender who works at Kahuna's in Malibu. His first name is Kalolo. Big guy, has a Marine tattoo on his left forearm. I'd like to know who he works for."

Donahue took out his phone and tapped something out. Notes, I presumed.

"Anything else?" he said.

"That'll do for now."

"Where can I reach you?"

I gave him my phone number.

"You'll hear from me before too long," Zane Donahue said. "I'm not a guy who likes to put things off. And I'm not a guy who likes to get turned down."

"I don't guess you are," I said.

He nodded. "We're going to have a good working relationship, I just know it."

SINCE I WAS already over on the Westside, I drove into Beverly Hills where the agency representing Lindsay DeSalvo was located. It was called Burlinson-Bainbridge on Canon Drive.

The first trick in Beverly Hills is to find a place on the street where you can park without paying a ransom or get a ticket for not having the right sticker in your window.

The building was two stories, flat and gray on the outside, with some sort of clinging vine around the door. Or maybe it was an actor trying to get in.

I pressed the buzzer and a woman's voice said, "Burlinson-Bainbridge."

"Yes, I have a question for you about one of your clients, Lindsay DeSalvo."

Pause. "What is this regarding?"

"I'm an investigator. I need to ask her a few questions. I can show you some ID."

"Is this a police matter?"

"Private."

Pause.

"Can you wait just a moment?" she said.

"I've got nothing but time," I said.

I leaned against the building and nodded to an older woman in a large, floppy hat as she walked her ferret of a dog. The fur ball paused to smell my foot and did not find it of interest. I could have told him that and saved him a sniff.

The voice came back.

"I'm sorry, sir, but we cannot give out any information to you."

"Are you taking your orders from Burlinson or Bainbridge?"

"Sir."

"Tell 'em I work for a lawyer," I said.

Pause.

"If you like, I can give you the number for our legal counsel."

"Who will give me the same runaround," I said.

"I'm sorry, sir."

"How about this," I said. "I give you a message for Lindsay, and you can get her the message, and she can call me."

Pause.

"I'm sorry, but that's all I can say at this point."

"You're sure that Burlinson or Bainbridge won't see me?"

"I'm really sorry."

"I'll audition," I said. "I'll do Hamlet's soliloquy. *O what a rogue and peasant slave am I.*"

Nothing.

I said, "Are you still there?"

She wasn't.

IT WAS NOW late morning and I was at the vortex of Los Angeles existence. Outward from Beverly Hills, in any direction, if you go far enough, you reach a dead end. Or the ocean. And in so doing you'll pass through a neighborhood with its own particular stamp. Ethnic or old money. On the way up or on the way down. Streets with potholes or newly paved. Free parking or metered. Strip malls or shopping plazas. Hopeless or hopeful. Angry or afraid or happily left alone.

And all of it run by chuckleheads with a private club in City Hall.

What a system.

I was about to head in a random direction when I got a call from Zane Donahue.

"What did I tell you?" he said. "Did I say soon or what?"

"What took you so long?"

Pause.

"Kidding," I said.

"What a guy," he said. "Where are you now?"

"Beverly Hills."

"Phony baloney."

"Help me find the real baloney."

"Gonna do it," he said. "Take PCH to Topanga Canyon. There's a place there where you're going to meet a guy."

"WELCOME TO THE Home of the First Heaven," the waitress said. She had perfect teeth in a smile inside a fresh, open face. She could have stepped out of a Norman Rockwell painting.

The Home of the First Heaven was an organic-only restaurant in the in the heart of Topanga Canyon. Zane Donahue sent me here, said I'd be provided with the information I was seeking. But it had to be done live and in person at this place.

Which was only fifteen minutes from the Cove.

The waitress said, "Can I start you off with some kale chips? A glass of wheat grass?"

"What do you like to eat here?" I said.

"My personal favorites?"

"Sure."

"I really love the four-bean mélange with tofu bread."

"Sounds great," I said. "Can you put some bacon on it?"

She reacted as if I'd slapped her.

"Kidding," I said.

"I'm glad," she said. "Do you know how bad that is for you?"

"Probably not," I said.

A quizzical look this time.

"I'm new in town," I said.

"From where?"

"Back east."

"Don't you just love it here?" she said.

"So far, so good," I said. "No earthquakes."

She giggled. "We're pretty safe here in the canyon."

"Maybe I should move here."

She raised her eyebrows. "Maybe you should."

"Tell you what," I said. "Bring me a cup of the four-bean thing. I'm also due to meet someone."

"No problem! Anything to drink?"

"I don't suppose you serve martinis."

"No alcohol."

"The moderate intake of alcohol is healthy," I said.

"You're kidding, right?"

I shook my head. "It cancels out the bacon."

She squinted.

"I'll just have some water," I said.

"Awesome sauce," she said.

"I'll have some of that, too."

She squinted again.

"Don't mind me," I said.

After she left I looked around at the other patrons in this first heaven eatery. Interesting name. The ancients had a view of levels of heaven, the sky being level number one. Behind that, who knows?

When I was a kid I used to look at the sky and the stars and imagine that instead of flaming gas they were alien search lights, looking for intelligent life and, spotting the earth, deciding to skip us.

I gave Sophie a call. The call went to voicemail. I left another message.

The waitress came back with my soup and water. I thought I was in a Warner Bros. prison movie from the '30s.

But I'll admit, the soup was heavenly. Maybe the place had a good rep for a reason. If they'd ever incorporate fried pork, they'd really be in business.

It was about five minutes after that when the guy arrived.

HIS RED BEARD was trimmed as neat as a toothbrush. He was in his thirties. He wore expensive black shoes and black slacks, a blue Oxford shirt open at the collar, and a dark-gray sport coat. He could have played the part of hipster lawyer or modeled for an Old Spice ad.

He sat in the chair opposite me. "I'm Robin," he said. He didn't offer his hand.

"Mike."

"I have some information for you."

I nodded.

"But first, something for you," he said. He took a white business-size envelope out of his inner coat pocket and handed it to me.

I looked inside. Five crisp $100 bills.

"A retainer," Robin said. "From the man we both work for."

"I don't work for him."

"Eventually, you will," Robin said.

The waitress appeared like a forest nymph and asked Robin if he'd like to see a menu.

"No, thanks," he said.

"You ought to order the awesome sauce," I said.

He looked at me. The waitress giggled.

"Some coffee," Robin said.

Off she went.

"I don't want to take any money," I said. "I did not agree to anything."

"But you'll want what I have to give you," Robin said. "This is a simple business transaction."

Five hundred bones was hard to ignore.

I said, "I retain the right to turn down a job I don't like. And return the money."

Robin nodded. "Mr. Donahue said that's exactly what you'd do. He's good that way."

"Apparently."

Coffee delivered, we were alone again. Robin took out his phone and thumbed it and looked at it, and occasionally at me, as he spoke. "The man you're interested in is Kalolo Tuputala. He tends bar, as you know, and hires out as private security. He's thirty-four years old, served four years in the Marine Corps. Did two tours in Afghanistan. Had a wife, Cecile, who committed suicide eight months after he came back. He got arrested and charged with felony vandalism a couple weeks later."

"When was this?"

"A little over five years ago," Robin said. "He went ex-vet nuts in a thrift store in Panorama City and broke all the china. Because of his service they knocked it down to a misdemeanor and probation. He got some treatments at the VA but then got hired as a bartender-slash-bouncer at a club in NoHo."

"How long has he been at Kahuna's?"

Robin looked at his phone. "Two years."

"You going to give me a copy of your notes?"

"No," Robin said. "When we finish here these get erased."

"That still isn't telling me much."

"We haven't got to the nut graph yet," Robin said. "Here it is. The most current security employment for Mr. Tuputala has been with Tanya Camarasa."

He paused.

I shrugged.

"She's a former NYU professor," Robin said, "who says she can talk to angels."

"SHE'S SERIOUS ABOUT it," Robin said. "And she has a bunch of people with her who are serious about it, too."

"Where?"

"A ranch called Peniel. Strange name, isn't it?"

"It's biblical," I said.

"Yeah?"

"It's the place where Jacob wrestled with God, and saw him face-to-face."

"You really know your stuff," Robin said. "Mr. Donahue said I'd be impressed, and I am. You need to join the team."

"I'm not a joiner."

"There will come a time when you need a team," Robin said.

"Where is this ranch?"

"You're in luck," Robin said. "It's only about two miles from here, up in the mountains. But I should tell you they're very shy. Invitation only."

"Maybe I'll invite myself."

"You could," Robin said, "if you knew where to enter."

He smiled in a knowing way. He and his employer were sure into knowing things.

The road Robin told me to take was lined with native grasses and brush. The SoCal coastal range is not easily habitable by man. Snakes and coyotes are more at home here. But it's a great place for hermits and antisocial types.

A gate with a heavy chain and lock and a *No Trespassing* sign stopped me. The road went on and around a bend. There was no sign of life or buildings.

I got out and hopped the gate.

A lizard the size of a Chicago hot dog scampered across the dirt path, paused to look at me, and hurried away. That's the way most people live, too—afraid, quick to scamper without deep thought.

I followed the path around a small jutting hill, and on the other side caught a nice vista of canyon, rock, and sky. This wasn't so bad out here. It would be prime location for any home developer, but of course it was protected by the state. And anyway, developments weren't scoring so well with the mad bomber on the loose.

Still no sign of man or beast. Only lizard and bird. And one ex-fighter trying to make a go of it as a finder of missing persons.

And then I heard some pounding.

Drums.

If this had been an Edgar Rice Burroughs or H. Rider Haggard novel—the kind my father read to me as a boy then I would have thought I was coming upon some ancient tribal ritual.

I followed the noise, and coming around one more turn, I could see in the distance a rag-tag jam session. Several people—men, women, boys, girls—banged different kinds of drums. Some of the drums were attached to bodies, some were on the ground. At least one of them was an overturned plastic bucket. The people were using hands and sticks to pound out what could only charitably be described as a rhythm.

In the middle of the semi-circle of percussionists were some people dancing to the improvised beat. By dancing, I don't mean Astaire. It was all waving arms and springy legs and bobble heads.

I stopped and watched for a moment from about forty yards away. Ecstatic dance has long been a staple of mystery religions, and if what I was walking into was Angel Talk Central, this might be considered business-as-usual.

On the outskirts of the gyration knot was a big guy with blond, curly hair. He turned and saw me and started to approach. He wore jeans and a black T-shirt with TOTO across the front of it. I wondered if that was for the band or the dog. Or maybe it was his name. I wasn't about to ask him.

"How you doin'?" he said. He had huge teeth in a mouth the size of a household trash compacter.

"What is this place?" I said.

"The place to be," he said.

"That's the place I'm looking for."

"Cool."

We looked at each other.

"Tell me more," he said.

"More?" I said.

"Why you're here."

"Oh, I was just hiking. Never been around here."

"Did you pass a *No Trespassing* sign?"

"I'm dyslexic," I said. "I thought it said *Gnissapsert On*."

His cave-sized mouth gaped.

"I need to ask you a question," he said.

"Shoot," I said.

"Are you with any governmental or law enforcement agency?"

It was a cool, practiced question. Completely useless, of course. People seem to think cops are not allowed to lie.

I said, "I wouldn't be an agent for any government, foreign or domestic."

"Very, very cool. Are you a journalist?"

"No way."

"Would you mind if I patted you down?" he said.

"I only get patted down by people I'm engaged to," I said. He scowled.

"Sure, go ahead," I said.

He gave me a once over like he was an ex-cop himself. I'd left my phone in the car and only had keys and a wallet.

"So what's going on here?" I said.

He turned to look at his drumbeating friends, then back at me. "What do you think of Earth?"

"I like it," I said.

"I mean, really. What is it to you?"

I pretended to think about it. "Well, I think we're doing a pretty bad job of keeping it clean. But there doesn't seem to be much we can do about that."

"You don't think so?"

"I wish there was."

Toto nodded and showed those teeth again. "There's someone I want you to meet. Come on."

He started walking, looked back to make sure I followed. I followed.

As we passed the drum and dancing corps I looked hard to see if Brooklyn might be there.

She wasn't.

TOTO TOOK ME up a twisting path, into a grove of native oaks and finally a clearing. In this clearing was a collection of tents.

"Welcome to Peniel," Toto said.

"Is this a campground?" I said.

"This property is actually owned by a winery. The owner lets us use it in return for some labor. He also believes in what we're doing."

"And what is that exactly?"

"Trying to save our only home, my friend, before it's too late."

We walked through the camp. It was set up with a main path through the middle. It reminded me of pictures of old mining camps I'd seen in books about the Old West. Or hippie communes that were the rage in the '60s. Outside one tent, sitting cross-legged, was a bearded guy in a wool hat sucking on a major blunt. The unmistakable odor of cannabis bit the air. Behind him, a little girl of seven or eight, barefoot and in a dirty pink dress, held a doll close to her and eyed me with suspicion.

The guy with the beard smiled and nodded at me.

At the end of this main path was another kind of tent. Huge. Right out of *Lawrence of Arabia*. Or what a well-heeled dad would rent out for his daughter's wedding reception.

The opening was spacious and I could see rugs and pillows inside, with a definite favoring of burgundy and gold.

Toto asked me to wait. He went in and stepped behind a cloth partition in the middle of the tent.

The drums were still pounding in the distance. It sounded like thunder.

A minute later, Toto came back and waved me into the tent.

THERE ARE PEOPLE who can take over a room just by walking in. They say Bill Clinton, once a president of the United States, was like that, and if you kept your hand on your wallet and locked up your daughter, you could appreciate the charisma.

I imagine some of the great stars of the golden age of movies were like that, too. Gable. Hepburn. Certain people the camera loves, and others have what used to be called *It*.

Something you feel immediately.

I was feeling it now.

She was medium height with hair like black satin. Her earrings were the size and sound of wind chimes. She wore a red silk pants suit, accented with a gold floral design. And no shoes. As to age, well, if there was a magazine that wanted to extol the beauty of women in their early fifties, she could have been their cover model.

With an incandescent smile she approached and put out her hand. "I'm Tanya."

"Mike," I said.

"Welcome to Peniel. Will you have tea with me?"

"I'm not much of a tea drinker," I said.

"You will be after tasting my blend," she said. She asked Toto to bring some and motioned for me to sit on a large, burgundy pillow with gold tassels. I parked myself on it. Tanya dropped elegantly onto a similar cushion and crossed her legs, yoga style.

She opened a silver box next to her pillow and took out three small sticks. Incense.

"Don't go to any trouble," I said.

"This is not trouble, Mike," she said. "This is an awakening."

She placed the sticks in a small, glass vase. From the box she removed a very plain lighter. That was kind of a letdown. I expected at least a turbaned eunuch with a candle to do the honors.

When the sticks were all infused with fire, tendrils of scented smoke curled toward me. I gave it a sniff.

"Not bad," I said.

"Lavender and frankincense," she said. "For your crown chakra. This will bring you into a consciousness of your own divine nature."

"I've been looking for that," I said. "I thought I misplaced it."

With a half smile she said, "You like to make light of things, don't you?"

"Laugh or die, that's my motto."

"I like it. We don't have enough laughter in our world, because we're choking to death on fumes."

Like this incense? I didn't say it.

"Now," she said, "what brings you to our community?"

"Well, Tanya. May I call you Tanya?"

She nodded.

"It started as just a hike, and I ran into some folks drumming away, and then started talking to that fellow, and it sounded interesting to me. So he brought me here. I'm kind of impressed."

She gave me the thoughtful eye of the lab researcher observing a rat. Then she said, "Do you believe in angels, Mike?"

Right to the heart of things. It was a quick, probing question and I knew she was going to listen carefully to my answer. Was I really who I said I was? Some random hiker? Or did I have an agenda?

"I guess that depends on what you mean by it," I said. "I've met some good people in my time."

"I'm talking about a race of beings we cannot see, unless they choose to be seen."

"Ah, incorporeal."

She seemed pleased. "You have an education."

"I read cereal boxes as a kid."

She laughed. It was an easy, attractive laugh. "I used to be a college professor, at NYU."

"No kidding."

"Until I discovered there is no truth there, not even a pretense of seeking the truth."

"I hear you," I said. I held up my left arm for her to read. She did. "Truth overcomes all?"

"Close enough," I said. "Impressive."

"*You* impress *me*. Tell me, do you believe in a spirit world?"

"I don't think you can rule it out," I said.

"Exactly! The utter pretentiousness of ignoring an entire realm of reality, simply because it cannot be measured or observed. That's what finally got to me in the academy."

"I guess the science people would ask how we know it's there if we can't see it."

"Can you see love, Mike? Can you photograph it? It's there, isn't it?"

"Good point. Angels, too?"

"Ah, but I have actually seen Michael. I have even seen Gabriel. And they have given me messages. My role in this life is to speak for them. I'm telling you, that is a much higher calling than trying to teach a bunch of naive freshmen to think."

"The hard part," I said, "is convincing people that you actually saw what you say you saw, heard what you heard."

"You are exactly right, Mike. Which is why I am prepared for this to take years. This is my preparation time, like John the Baptist. Right now I am a voice crying in the wilderness."

"Sounds positively biblical," I said.

"No, the Bible is old news. Ancient. It has been used to justify humankind's rape of Earth. The angels are not pleased by this. Not at all."

"Why do you call this place Peniel, then?"

"Because this is where I wrestle with God."

"With God himself?"

"*Herself*, Mike. Ah, here's our tea."

TOTO PLACED A silver tray on the floor. It had two cups with steel tea infusers in them, and a pot in the middle. Toto said nothing and left.

I followed Tanya's lead, took the infuser out and lifted the cup. It was like we were toasting.

I took a small sip. It tasted like old bog.

"I like it," I said.

"It's made from a native flower and my own selection of herbs," she said.

"You sell this?"

She shook her head. "That would be prostitution."

She drank some more, waited for me to do the same. I faked a sip.

"What do you do for a living, Mike?"

"I'm sort of in the ranks of the unemployed right now," I said.

"What kind of work have you done in the past?"

"Odd jobs, here and there."

"Somebody with your education and intelligence?"

"Not a lot of permanent positions for philosophy majors."

"There might be here," she said. "For you."

"Is this a job interview?"

"Mike, there is a global movement and awakening to what's happening to Earth. The problem in the past is that people have tried to make things happen to stop it. What we've failed to realize is that we are being called upon not to act, but to react."

I nodded as if I was interested.

"Over a billion years ago," she said, "angels came out of Earth and became guardians of it."

Instead of snorting, I forced myself to take another sip of tea.

"You don't believe this?" she said.

"I don't know anything about it," I said.

"Of course not. It has not been revealed to us until these latter times."

"Angels did the revealing?"

"The archangel Michael," she said. "He came to me in a vision, Mike. Right out there, about a hundred feet from where we're sitting."

"What did he look like?" I asked.

"Very big and very strong, and glowing."

"Did he have wings?"

"That's just in children's stories," she said.

"Did he introduce himself?"

"The first thing he said to me was, 'Do not be afraid.' And then he told me that the time was coming when those who love Earth must be gathered."

"Which is what this is," I said, making a roundhouse gesture with my arm. Which suddenly felt very heavy.

"Yes," she said.

"Did you hear about the explosion near the ..."

"Near the ...?"

I couldn't remember. It was there somewhere in the thick broth that was my brain. A broth that smelled like lavender and frankincense and something else.

"Getty ..." I said.

She just looked at me.

"And the ... website, talks about Michael ..."

Her face started to blur. The tendrils of incense smoke, which had been blowing my way the whole time, become hands. A thumb and forefinger closed my nose. My head started its own drum circle behind my eyes.

I think I mumbled something that sounded like *pastrami*. And then I was in dreamland.

IT STARTED OFF as a pleasant dream. Somebody was playing acoustic guitar and there was a sunrise coming up over the mountains. A horse walked over to me and snorted, then turned into a plane. A hatch opened up and a conveyor belt was dropped and luggage started coming out. The luggage all looked exactly the same.

Then Sean Connery slid down the belt. It was the Sean Connery of Indiana Jones. He looked at me and said, "Trouble?"

My dream self stood mute.

The plane had propellers. They started to go around and round. I was walking into them. I tried to stop myself but I kept moving forward, almost like I was on a belt myself. Then the propeller started on my face.

It stung but it did not kill me.

Again and again and again.

Then I woke up.

Somebody was slapping me.

"He's coming around," somebody said.

Whoever was standing over me working on my face had onion breath.

"Hit him with the ice," a distant voice said.

Two men.

My eyes were just making out Claude, the muscle from Jon-Scott Morrow's beach house, when he dumped a bucket of ice water on me.

That's when I realized I was tied to a chair, clad only in my briefs.

The shock to my system did its work and my nerves went on full alert.

Shaking the water from my face, I tensed to find out where the major restraints were. My arms were behind me and there were several loops of rope around me. Tight. They knew their work.

The room was cold and windowless and dark except for a single light bulb attached to a low ceiling. "How you doing there, Bambi?" Onion-breath Claude had his face right in front of mine.

Bambi?

"Who's your girlfriend?" I said.

"I love the way you talk," Claude said.

"Get on with it," the other guy said. "I want some steak."

The voice sounded familiar.

He appeared out of the shadows, behind Claude's right shoulder.

Kalolo the bartender.

"Hurry up," Kalolo said.

"What's your rush?" Claude said.

"I'm hungry."

"Yeah you are."

"Let's all go grab a burger," I said. "Talk this out."

"You love to talk," Claude said.

"Communication's a beautiful thing," I said.

"Who do you work for?"

"UPS," I said.

Claude gave me four knuckles to my face. Fireworks exploded behind my eyes.

"Don't tell me," Claude said. "I like doing this."

When one is secured to a chair and is outnumbered by a two-thug ratio, there are only a couple of options. First option is to figure out a way to do the movie thing and take down said thugs with a one-in-a-thousand move. That move usually includes whatever the good guy is connected to.

It would help if one of the too-stupid-to-live bad guys walked out, leaving only one thug to finish the job. Then by way of head butt or groin kick, good guy disables his one adversary and goes after the other one.

The second option is find a vulnerability in the thug's ego. The odds of this working are only slightly better than the first. But having two bad choices, you go with the least bad, just like in politics.

I had an advantage. I'd dealt with both these boys before.

Kalolo was not going to be interested in my proposals. I'd already shamed him, but privately. He just wanted me dead.

Claude, on the other hand, I'd controlled in front of his boss, or his lover, or whoever Jon-Scott Morrow was to him. He'd almost cried.

He was the one to concentrate on.

"You only like hitting somebody who can't move," I said. "There's a name for somebody like that."

"I'd love to take you apart," Claude said.

"You couldn't do it if I was out of this chair."

"Forget that," Kalolo said. "Let me cut him up, will you?"

"Hold on," Claude said. "This guy wants a piece of me."

"Fair fight," I said. "You can even have your girlfriend hold a gun on me. Just as long as we make it fair."

"You got no bargaining power," Claude said.

"You're dying to know if you can take me," I said. To Kalolo I said, "You got a piece on you?"

He said nothing.

Claude said, "Where's your piece?"

"Come on!" Kalolo said.

"Where is it?"

"I got it. Here." Kalolo pulled a gun from the back of his pants.

"Hold it on him," Claude said. "If he takes me out, shoot him."

"This isn't how it's supposed to go down," Kalolo said.

"Shut up!" Claude said. "Do what I tell you."

"You got nothing to lose," I said to the bartender. "After I take care of Onion Breath there, you and I can dance again."

"I got onion breath?" Claude said.

SO HE UNTIED me. Kalolo stood about ten yards away, gun at the ready.

"So where is this place?" I said, rubbing my wrists.

"Hell," Claude said.

"That's really bad dialogue," I said. "You've been hanging out with the wrong people."

"You know you're not getting out of here alive, right? No matter what happens."

"Hell would be an eternity having to listen to you," I said. "So are you going to make it a fair fight?"

"Sure," Claude said. "Anytime you're ready."

"Let me loosen up a little."

Claude answered that by executing a roundhouse kick. A pretty good one. I ducked it.

"Hold it," I said. "I'm not ready."

Back he came, a rush job, fists flying. I parried each blow then pushed him over my leg. Down he went.

"Time out!" I said.

"Ain't no time out!" Kalolo said.

"I just called it," I said. "Don't you guys know how to play?"

"Let me shoot this—" and he finished off with four-syllable word that is both unoriginal and the mark of the unintelligent.

"You don't do nothin'," Claude said.

I said, "I'm just trying to get the rules straight."

"Ain't gonna be no rules," Claude said.

"Then I may just as well go home," I said.

It was the look of consternation and confusion that the two thugs exchanged that almost made this whole thing worthwhile. You have to pick your moment, and this was mine. I open palmed the lightbulb and everything went dark.

A shot fired. I felt it whiz by my left ear.

In the darkness Claude shouted, "Don't shoot!"

His voice gave me a reading. I gave the left-heel jab to chest level and got a satisfactory thud. Claude was going down again. I followed my foot and led with my knees. They pile-drived into his body. I found his face with my hand and thumbed his right eye. He screamed. I broke his nose with my right elbow.

I immediately went into a roll and found my chair. Now it was a weapon. I grabbed the back and held it in front of me like a bull's horns.

And listened.

Instead of being quiet, like he should've been, Kalolo made all sorts of desperate puffing noises. I rushed at the noises with the chair.

The next sound he issued was the kind you make when you're impaled. I pulled the chair back and brought it down on where I guessed his head was. The chair did not break like in the old cowboy movies. But his head probably did.

I sensed him falling to the ground. I jumped on him. He didn't resist. He was out. I felt along his arm and found his hand and gun. I removed the gun, a revolver, and stood.

It wasn't hard to get a bead on Claude in the dark. He was snuffling and groaning.

I patted Kalolo's pockets. Took out his phone. Found an *On* key.

The room filled with dim, dark-blue light.

The screen said *Swipe screen to unlock.*

I swiped.

More light. No password necessary. Lazy bartenders make the best informants.

I turned the screen toward Claude.

Who was lying on the ground, touching his face.

"How do I get out, Claude?" I said.

He didn't say anything.

I pressed the gun to his head.

"Don't shoot, come on!" he said.

"Are we alone in this place?" I said.

"Yes!"

"If you lie to me, Claude, I'll have to use this."

"I'm bleeding here!"

"Where are we, Claude? And remember not to lie to me. I don't like that."

Silence.

I fired a shot into the wall.

Claude yelped.

"A place we use!" he said.

"*Where?*"

"Nearby. On the side of the hill."

"Anybody outside?"

"No."

"Don't lie to me, Claude."

"I'm not! I swear!"

"Just you and your girlfriend?"

"Stop calling him that."

"Save your indignation, Claude."

"My what?"

"You depress me, Claude. And you've made me really mad. So I'm going to ask you once, who told you to bring me here and what were you supposed to do to me?"

"You're gonna kill me, so why should I say anything?"

"I don't murder people, Claude. Unless it's a Friday. Is it Friday?"

"Are you serious?"

"Talk to me, Claude."

"I don't think I want to."

In the light of the phone he looked like a petulant child.

I fired a shot at Claude's feet.

He yipped and said, "We were supposed to find out who you're working for, that's all."

"Then kill me?"

Claude said nothing.

"Because you and your platonic friend here murder any day of the week, yes?"

Silence.

An arm the size of a log wrapped around my throat.

THERE ARE CERTAIN things you can do only if you've

been trained in both body and mind. And there are other things you can do only if your mind is wired a certain way. That's the wild card.

I've been in the cage with fighters that had the goods, physically and mentally. But their native brains lacked the spark that was, for some reason, given to me. A spark that lets me see things instantly and react to them.

I knew that the other arm behind me was going to pull my gun hand in less than a quarter second. That's the time it took me to fire a round into Claude's gut before it happened.

Kalolo hit it hard, my arm, enough to dislodge the gun.

Now all I had to do was get a giant Pacific Islander arm off my throat before I passed out.

I dropped the phone and used both hands to pull down on his arm, getting a little flow of air.

Then I pushed with my legs like I was a soccer goalie reaching for a high shot. We fell backwards. I was on top of him now, my back on his front. A couple of spoons, an image which to this day I long to delete.

The only things I had were my elbows.

Nobody knows for sure when elbow fighting became a disciplined art. It has probably been around for three millennia. I'm sure it didn't take the smartest Sumerian to figure out that crushing somebody's face with the sharp bone in the middle of their arm was an effective maneuver.

But it was probably the Cambodians who took it to the next level and made an art out of it. *Bokator* they called it. *To strike a lion.*

This was part of my own training. I like elbows a lot.

Getting the strikes to affect the bartender was difficult because of his layer of fat. I concentrated on his right side, giving ten strikes in about five seconds.

The arm around my throat weakened. I busted out of it and reversed on top of him.

I was about to hammer his head *bokator* style when another of those instant messages hit my brain.

I grabbed as much of Kalolo as I could and rolled, pulling him on top of me just as the gun fired twice.

MATH HAS ALWAYS come easily to me. I have no problem subtracting four from six. Kalolo had fired one shot. I'd done three. If the revolver was a six-shooter, which was likely, there were two slugs in the mighty bulk of Kalolo the bartender, one inside Claude, and nothing left in the cylinder.

But there was a ton of Samoan on top of me.

I heard scuffling. And moaning. I used a submission-defense move to squirm out from under the thankfully motionless body.

In the dim I saw Claude holding the gun like a hammer, about to use my head as the nail.

I banked right but he got my shoulder.

Steel hurts.

Claude fell on me.

He screamed and spit at my face.

With the heel of my palm I jammed his chin and felt his jaw unhinge.

I followed that with the hammer, my rock, my right fist, aimed at the silhouette of Claude's head.

He went night-night.

And with the bullet hole in him, he was not going to be waking up.

It sure felt like Friday. Dark-night-of-the-soul Friday. Killing does that. This darkness sticks to your ribs and squeezes your heart and your lungs.

It keeps you up at night.

THE PLACE WAS dark again. I felt around for the phone, found it. Lit the place up once more.

Kalolo was dead.

Claude, too.

He'd been the last one to fire the gun. It was lying next to him.

I picked it up by the trigger guard, then used Claude's shirt to give the butt and trigger a rubdown. Then I put it Claude's hand and wrapped his fingers around the butt and put his index finger on the trigger. He had plenty of residue on him.

I looked around for my clothes. Not there. I had to kick open the door of this hobbit room. There was a small passage with light coming in at the end. I saw a crude, wooden set of steps leading up to a flat door.

I stepped up and pushed the door open a crack and looked out.

I was on hill covered with cornstalk-colored weeds. I clambered out of the chamber and into the sun.

I was alone on a hill that was itself alone. Which was good, considering there were two dead bodies below me and I was clad only in briefs.

Life's embarrassing situations.

The only other sign of human imprint were two small solar panels next to the door. Somebody had gone to a great deal of trouble to create this place, with solar power and a generator for light and air.

I figured I was not far from the camp. My car was still parked out there, probably being watched. I hated to do it, but I decided to leave Spinoza for now.

Using Kalolo's phone, I called Ira.

"I'm in my underwear on a hill," I said.

"I always knew you'd end up that way," he said.

"It's going to get cold soon. And I may not be alone for long."

"Wait a second, you're serious?"

"I need some backup," I said. "I'm going to work my way around to where I can't be seen."

"Probably a good thing."

"If I leave the phone on, can you triangulate and find out where I am?"

"Where's your car?"

"Probably being watched. Or worked over."

"By whom?"

"Tell you when you get here."

IN TEN MINUTES Ira called me back and told me I was near a fire road, and he could be there in an hour.

Traffic permitting, of course.

The air was taking a definite turn toward chill. Dark clouds, something Southern Cal hadn't seen a lot of lately, gathered on the horizon. There was a hint of salt in the air, not surprising since I was in a canyon that funneled to the ocean. That mix of sun and cool air makes these hills ideal for vineyards. There's a bunch of them up here. Only not near me. Too bad. I could've used a nice glass of Cabernet.

I sat behind some brush just in case a deer should happen by. Nothing like a guy in his underwear to spook the local fauna.

And started checking the contents of Kalolo's phone. There was a list of contacts that Ira could check later, cross referencing them with some database or other. I'm sure we'd get a list of felons that might prove to be a haystack with maybe one needle in it.

His call history had a good list that we could check, too.

What interested me most were his photos and videos.

There's nothing visually worse than a thug's selfie. His gallery was stuffed with them. A lot of them with customers, some of them with girls who frankly looked like just the kind who would love punks like this guy. The old bad boy syndrome that never works out.

I went through about a hundred photos until I got tired of seeing this guy's face.

There was a folder marked Vids and I tried to get in. It asked for a password. The content was enough for even a lazy bartender to protect. It would take some of Ira's magic to gain access.

It was going on twenty minutes since Ira had called.

Sitting there like early man on the plains of the Serengeti, I almost laughed. There's all this technology in the palm of my hand. And over here is me, in my loin cloth, facing the elements with nothing but attitude.

And then I found myself thinking of my old buddy C Dog again. Why did he keep popping up in my thoughts?

Because you want to save him. Because maybe in saving him you are staking out a claim that there is really a meaningful existence for you, for him, for anybody. Maybe that's the way you deal with having blood on your hands. It doesn't wash off with water, metaphorical or otherwise. You can only cover it up. So that's why you do these things for other people.

And what's wrong with that? If it gets you going and keeps you from slicing your wrists, that's a plus.

A rustling in the scrub got my attention. I look toward the sound. The sound stopped. I kept my eyes on the spot, but otherwise didn't move.

And then I saw it, looking at me through the brush. A rabbit. Its black eyes set in gray fur was giving me the once over.

Take a good look, Bunny. You're probably happier right where you are. Stay away from hunters and hawks, and you'll be all right.

I remembered then the only time I ever went hunting.

My mom had shipped me off to spend a few days with her

father, my grandfather. I had not seen him much growing up and I was excited to go. He had a place in northern Indiana that sounded like something out of one of my adventure stories.

It turned out I was not far wrong. He lived in a small house with a lot of property around it, close to a wood.

Harold Broxton was a big man. I remember he had enormous hands that felt like dry leather when we shook. He'd been in the Navy in World War II, grew up in the Depression when hunting for his family was not an option but a necessity. I always sensed there was some tight wire of tension between him and his daughter. But that was covered by her obvious love for him. My grandfather, on the other hand, was not one to show emotion.

I wanted to be like him. I wanted to be big and I didn't want to be the emotional basket case I usually was. So when he said he was going to take me hunting, I was excited. We were going to go out like Daniel Boone and I could prove my manhood, which I hoped was lurking inside me somewhere.

He got me up while it was still dark. I remember the breakfast, bacon and eggs. In the cold of the house and sleep still in my eyes, the bacon and eggs tasted like the best thing in the world. As we ate, he talked to me man to man.

"We're going to spend a couple of hours with the rifle. I'm going to teach you how to shoot a .22. Then you'll practice with it. I have set targets for you. Tomorrow, we will have another morning like this and will go out and hunt some rabbits. How does that sound?"

It sounded like H. Rider Haggard to me. The fat kid was going to get some training in the fine art of manliness.

The training with the rifle was exhilarating. Grandpa showed me how to load a bullet into the bolt-action, single-shot chamber. He showed me how to use the sight. And finally let me shoot it.

"Don't pull the trigger," he said. "Squeeeze it."

When I fired that first shot, and that shot hit the round target in the bullseye, I thought for one moment, one small slice of my youth, that I really could learn to do anything and be anybody. That there was hope for me yet.

The two hours of target practice, mixed with a snack of beef jerky and lemonade, made the perfect morning.

Until the next one, when we went out to hunt.

WE GOT TO a clearing in the woods where the morning sun was just hitting the dew on the grass. Grandpa walked slowly, eyes ahead, and I copied his every move.

Mighty hunter. I wanted to be just like him.

And then he stopped, put up his hand for me to stop too. He pointed.

There it was, a gray bunny, sniffing the ground.

Grandpa made a motion for me to shoot.

Adrenaline rush. I put the rifle up and got the rabbit in my sights, just like he'd taught me.

Squeeeeze.

Blam.

A burst of fur. A small spot of red.

And the rabbit started running—no, limping!—away.

"You need to finish him," Grandpa said.

"Huh?" I was suddenly horrified at what I'd done.

"It's suffering! Go find it and kill it!"

Looking back over the span of time, I know that Grandpa was teaching me what a hunter needed to know. But at ten it sounded like the worst thing in the world. Find. Kill. Because I had put a bullet in a rabbit and it was still alive.

"Now!" Grandpa shouted.

Gorge rising in my throat, I ran after the rabbit.

It didn't take long to find. It had stopped running. It lay on its side, unable to move, but still breathing. Panting.

And the eye of the rabbit, the smooth, cold, and terrified eye, looked up at me.

I froze.

Grandpa yelled, "Find it?"

Tears in my eyes now. "Yes!"

"Alive?"

"Yes!"

"Shoot it!"

Bawling, I put another bullet in my rifle.

I put the rabbit in my sights.

And couldn't shoot. I could not shoot the rabbit that was looking in abject fear.

"Now!" Grandpa shouted.

I put the muzzle to the head and turned my own head away.

And pulled, not squeezed, the trigger.

I could not look.

I ran back to my grandfather, ashamed that I was crying, that I was no hunter. That I was a failure.

He left me there in silence, went to put the rabbit in his hunting sack.

When he got back, bless his memory, he put his arm around me and walked me to the car and said, "You did right, Michael. And you never have to go hunting again."

Never again did I hunt.

But I've killed.

I CAME OUT of my memory, and saw that the rabbit was long gone.

And I was colder than ever.

The phone rang. Ira calling back.

"I'm almost there," he said. "Where's your car?"

"Probably being watched or handled by people with drums."

"With what?"

"Never mind. You've got some work to do."

"Paid?"

"Challenging."

"What I figured. Over and out."

His van pulled into sight five minutes later. I made my way down the hill and got in. Ira reached behind and grabbed a blanket, tossed it to me.

Then he said, "I'm ready for your explanation now."

"You want the short version or the long version?"

"Long, of course," Ira said.

I said, "I'll give you the in between. I got set up. By a guy named Zane Donahue. Ever heard of him?"

"I don't think so."

"He's of the criminal element, let's put it that way. I went to him to get information on this bartender."

"Which bartender?"

"The one I killed."

Ira said, "Oh no."

"You want the story or not?"

He was silent.

"I had to kill the bartender and another guy—"

"You *what?*"

My voice rose of its own accord. "It had to be done. And now I've got this phone, see, and we need to get into it. There's a video, but it's password protected."

"We'll get it," Ira said. "Shall we get your car?"

"Wait until it's darker," I said.

"You just want to sit here?"

"For now," I said.

"Then please tell me everything," Ira said.

I did, starting with the awesome sauce.

BY THE TIME I finished, it was moving toward dark.

"Let's find Spinoza," I said. "You bring any weaponry?"

"Only my wits," Ira said.

"I'm comforted."

It took us fifteen minutes to work around to the road where I'd left my car. Still there. We came up slowly, lights off. Ira stopped about thirty yards away and we both watched for movement in the fading light.

Seeing none I got out and walked to my ride.

He has looked better.

His black ragtop had a mean gash and the passenger side window was shattered.

I looked in the glove compartment. The envelope with the five hundred dollars was gone.

Since I didn't have the key, I hot-wired Spinoza and drove to Ira's. I took a shower and got dressed in a pair of Ira's well-worn sweats. They were tight but did the trick.

"You look like an uncomfortable sausage," Ira said when I joined him in the living room.

"That's exactly what I am," I said. "A bunch of inedible humanity wrapped in a skin."

"Inedible?"

"I killed two people today."

"Who were going to kill you," Ira said.

"It keeps happening."

"You go into dangerous places, you run into dangerous people."

"It's not like I want to."

"Ah, but the world itself is getting more dangerous."

"It's always been dangerous," I said.

"Less so when there was a genuine fear of God in abundance. Remember, it is the fear of God which is the beginning of wisdom. So as society proceeds in the removal of that basis for moral behavior, what do you get?"

"Reality TV."

"That, and the unloosing of man's natural tendency toward evil."

"Am I evil?" I said.

"Do you think you are?"

"I've broken the commandment, thou shalt not kill."

"It's actually thou shalt not murder," Ira said. "You've not murdered anyone."

"What about New Haven?"

I'd told Ira of the man I'd killed a couple of years after my parents were gunned down in that Yale shooting. The shooter was a student named Blackpoole, but he'd been turned into a killer under the influence of one Thurber McDaniels. My father, a philosophy professor at Yale, had caught McDaniels in a clear case of plagiarism. That got McDaniels kicked out. He gathered a small group of disciples around an obscure nihilistic philosophy from ancient China. My theory was that McDaniels used drugs and mind control to get Blackpoole to do his deed then kill himself. I found Thurber McDaniels and confronted him with this. His answer was to try to slice me up with a samurai sword. I knocked him out, he hit his head on a table, hard. He didn't move. My mind on fire, I used the sword to finish him.

Only Ira knows about this.

"As your lawyer," Ira said, "I would argue that the blow to the head killed him, making it self-defense. Even if it was the sword, that would be heat-of-passion."

"None of that's going to help me sleep better."

"Which is a sign that your heart is not cold, and that you are not evil."

"Maybe I'd rather sleep."

Ira shook his head. "There are some bargains we dare not take."

I SLEPT BETTER than I thought I would.

I woke up to the smell of Ira's cooking. He called it *shak-shuka*, and it made me almost believe in goodness again. After we ate, Ira went to work on cracking the videos in Kalolo's phone.

Dressed like an uncomfortable sausage again, with a pair of old flip-flops, I made one last attempt to get to Sophie. I walked to the Argo.

The guy behind the counter was college-age and trying hard to grow a goatee, and failing.

"Help you?" he said.

"I'm a friend of Sophie's," I said.

He gave me a long look.

"Oh ... kay," he said.

"I've been trying to get in touch with her. We were supposed to get together."

"She's not here."

"She doesn't seem to be answering her phone."

"Wish I could help," Goatee said.

"Do you?"

His eyelids did a little dance.

"Can I leave her a message?" I said.

"Um ..."

"On a piece of paper."

Goatee looked to the side, like an actor who forgot his lines seeking the prompter in the wings.

A moment later, out from a cubicle, the owner of the store emerged. I'd seen him before, in the background. He was around seventy and looked like a man who sat a lot. He came over and stood next to Goatee.

"Can I help you find something?" the owner said.

"Sophie," I said. "I'm a friend."

"Ah." He stepped from around the counter and placed his hand on my arm, turning me. I let him. He walked me to a far aisle—the self-help section as it turned out—where we could be alone.

"I know who you are," he said.

"It's mutual," I said.

"It would be best if you didn't try to contact Sophie."

"Why would that be best?" I said.

"Trust me," he said.

"I need more than that," I said.

"Please, she does not want to see you."

"She told you that?"

He nodded. "And I'd like to ask you not to come into the store when she's working."

"I like this store."

"Please leave," he said

"This is not exactly good customer relations," I said.

"I'm sorry," he said.

I walked out.

IRA WAS IN his wheelchair, facing the door. Like he'd been waiting for me.

"You might need to sit down for this," Ira said.

"I don't want to sit down," I said, still steaming from the encounter at the store.

"Michael, I'm sorry."

He said it like there was a death in the family.

He wheeled himself to the computer. I came up behind him.

"I'll start it from the beginning," Ira said. He hit a key and a video began playing.

It showed feet. Walking. The camera operator, who I assumed was Kalolo Tuputala, was following along. The lighting was minimal. Twilight. Or early morning. The pairs of feet were crunching the ground. It was sandy and rocky.

The camera stopped moving and panned up.

It was a big man with a large bag or tarp over his shoulder. We only saw his back.

He stopped and took the package off his shoulder, lowered it to the ground.

Then he turned back toward the camera.

It was Claude.

He waved at the camera to come over. As it did, he opened up the package.

The camera moved in.

On the face of Brooklyn Christie.

Acid rose to the back of my throat.

Ira put his hand on my arm.

The video went on.

Claude dragged Brooklyn into a hole.

A grave.

The video ended.

Now I sat. Heavily. In a chair by the window. Out there somewhere, the body of a dead girl I'd been hoping was alive. Out there, her father hoping the same thing. I knew how this would hit him. I'd been there, big time, double time, my parents, and all of those feelings came together inside me then, a black ball of ice-cold emptiness.

I don't know how long I sat there staring before I turned back to Ira. He was at the computer again, looking at the monitor.

"Come look at this," he said.

"Forget it," I said.

"No, you need to see."

I walked over. Ira had paused the video on a frame that had a horizon shot in it. The sky was either going to dark or dawn. There was a burnt-orange hue to it.

Silhouetted against the sky was a rock formation, something that looked like the prow of a ship.

Ira said, "There is one place that has a formation like that."

"Where?"

"About an hour and a half from here. In the desert. A place called Vasquez Rocks."

"You don't think we could—"

"I'm ahead of you. Give me some time and I might be able to pinpoint where this video was shot."

I walked out to the backyard and sat on the bench under Ira's magnolia tree. I tried to console myself with the thought that finding Brooklyn's body and getting it to her father would at least give him some closure.

At the same time, I tried not to think of Sophie.

I didn't have much luck on either count.

I lay down on the bench and put my arm over my eyes.

Then I heard Ira's voice from inside. "Michael! Let's go!"

"VASQUEZ ROCKS," IRA said as he drove us in his van, "is where a bandit named Vasquez used to hide."

"Now that's a coincidence," I said.

Ira sighed. "It's a park now, but the place we're going is outside those limits."

The traffic on the freeway heading north was light. A nice change from the L.A. norm.

"And if we find her," Ira said, "we go to the sheriff with it. They have jurisdiction out here."

"Keep me out of it," I said.

"That may not be possible," Ira said.

"Think of something. You always do."

"Right now I'm thinking of you. Cooperating with the law is not always a bad thing."

I looked out the window at a row of tract homes lit up by street lights.

Ira said, "You never completed your story, about what happened back in New Haven. Why you're on the lam, so to speak."

"Another time," I said.

"We've got twenty more minutes of driving. No time like the present."

"How 'bout those Dodgers?"

Ira sighed. We said nothing through the Newhall Pass. On the other side, a bright sun lit up the sky.

"See that?" Ira said.

"See what?"

"The sun is pumping fire. As long as the sun pumps fire, there's hope. It's like a beating heart."

"You're awfully poetic today."

He smiled. Knowingly. I hate it when he does that. It's like he knows something about *me*. He's usually right.

IRA PULLED OFF the freeway, pointing to Vasquez Rocks in the distance. He drove a couple of miles and then turned right on a two-lane blacktop. Another mile to a dirt road. He took that until we came to a smaller road. I could tell from the look on Ira's face that he really wanted this to work. This whole thing was a challenge for him.

I was hoping it would work for another reason. At least we could give Ray Christie his daughter's body so he could give her a proper burial.

We veered off the road onto raw desert and stopped about twenty yards in. He opened up his laptop, looked at it for thirty seconds. "It should be here," he said. "Let's have a look."

"You're going to look too?"

"I didn't drive all the way out here to be a spectator." He grabbed his forearm crutches and let himself out of a van.

I got out on the other side.

"You don't have to do this," I said.

"I need the workout," Ira said. He made a circle motion with one of his crutches. "It is somewhere in this general area. Let's move in opposite directions about fifty yards, then make a square of fifty. We'll tighten it inward after that."

I marveled at Ira's strength as he propelled himself with the crutches along the path he had chosen. I did the same going the other way.

The desert in November is not a bad place to be. There's a beauty to it. As long as you don't step on the wrong creature.

The ground was all rock and sand, with one Joshua tree in the middle of the square we were marking. I could see the big rock formations in the distance. It looked like Mars in an old science fiction movie. Reminded me of when I borrowed *A Princess of Mars* from the library when I was a kid. And the part where John Carter is brought into this massive building where the artificial atmosphere of Mars is created and pumped out. A ray of the sun is harnessed and combined with electric vibrations. Technology is what makes life possible on Mars.

I wondered if Dr. Gary Pasfield had ever read the book. I was thinking of that little biosphere he had on his desk, growing parsley.

As I was letting my mind wander around like my feet, I heard Ira call.

"I found it," he said.

I JOGGED OVER. He was standing next to a mound of dirt, slightly discolored. As if someone had tried to move the sand around to blend everything, but hadn't quite made it.

We looked at each other.

"Go get the shovel," Ira said.

This was the second grave I'd dug up in a year's time. I was getting good at it. Not a skill you want to have, unless you're a Marine or a method actor preparing to play the gravedigger in *Hamlet*. Ira told me to go gently, so I wouldn't disturb the body.

It was dismal work. Ira has been around his share of death, much of it inflicted by himself. Other deaths falling around him. He told me once you never get used to it. You get cold, you get hard, but somewhere inside you there's a corrosion. You may not even feel it until years later when a big chunk of your soul falls off.

I was beginning to listen to his talk about a soul. Something about that kept nagging at me.

I dug for about five minutes before I hit something hard. A rock?

No.

It was a knee.

More digging, more exposure. She had been buried naked. Just like in the video.

When I got to where the head would be I used my hands to clear away the dirt. I kept thinking of poor Ray Christie and how this was going to hit him. The man put all his hopes on reconciliation with his daughter. And it was too late. What would she look like when he viewed her? I hope he would see in her a little bit of the little girl he once knew.

But that was not going to happen.

Not now, at least.

Because the face did not belong to Brooklyn Christie.

"NOT HER?" IRA said.

"No."

"Then who?"

"Her name is Lindsay DeSalvo," I said.

"And you know this how?"

"She was a friend of Brooklyn's."

"But the woman in the video …"

"That was Brooklyn, no question."

"Then how?"

I started spitballing. "What if they switched the bodies?"

"For what purpose?" Ira said.

"You tell me," I said.

"There was no other footage on that video," Ira said. "At least that I found."

"Why record it at all?"

"Visual proof," Ira said.

"For who?"

"That's the right question," Ira said, "but we're in no position to know, even if that's our working theory."

"Think about it," I said, "as we look for another grave."

WE SPENT THE next half hour combing every rock and pebble and tumble-weed-laced patch of that ground. And found nothing like a grave or a mound or a discoloration of ground.

And as bad as I felt for Lindsay DeSalvo, a little part of me wondered if Brooklyn might still be alive. That Kalolo and Claude had tried to pull a fast one on someone who wanted Brooklyn dead.

It was a stretch. But I felt like stretching.

The sun was giving off some heat now. In the distance I could see a truck rumbling along the two-lane blacktop, and a sedan of some kind going the other way.

Ira said, "It's time to notify the sheriff's office in Palmdale. They need to take over. Are you ready?"

"For what?"

"To tell them how we happen to be the ones who found the body."

"A song and dance?" I said.

"Be nice," Ira said.

IT TOOK A full hour before a sheriff's vehicle arrived. Two deputies took an initial report from Ira. I sat in his van, on the passenger side, with the door open. Half an hour later, a homicide investigator, a deputy named Givins, showed. He was early forties and had a lean and hungry look. Such men are dangerous. Shakespeare taught us that.

Ira showed him a credential that Givins took to his car. He made a radio call, returned the credential and spoke once more to Ira.

While he did that, I tried to make sense of the body-switch theory. Brooklyn could have been drugged. She could have been knocked out. They made the video, started throwing dirt on her.

But that's when the video ended.

She also could be dead and buried somewhere else.

That last thought hit me hard. What if she was never found?

This would hurt Ray Christie worst of all. I started to wonder if it would be better to know she was dead than never know for sure.

When it was all over Ira was driving us back. He told me we'd meet with them in a few days, turn over the phone, and tell them everything.

"Not everything," I said.

"How's that?" Ira said.

"We don't know the ending yet."

Ira drove in silence for a few minutes, then said, "That poor girl."

"Lindsay DeSalvo."

"Any motive you see?"

"Just that—" Some tumblers clicked into place in my brain. I sat up straight.

"What is it?" Ira said.

"A connection. Between Lindsay and Claude and—"

"Who's Claude?"

"One of the guys I left up there in the hills."

"Ah. And there's a third person?"

"Maybe," I said.

"And who would that be?"

"Would you believe Wild Bill Hickok?"

A LITTLE AFTER midnight, back at the Cove, I jogged along the dark Pacific's edge.

This was not exercise.

It took me about ten minutes to reach my destination. The ski mask and crowbar I held like a baton did not slow me down.

Jon-Scott Morrow's beach house had a security system. I'd noticed it when I first encountered his fat butt ten days ago.

I was going to have to move fast.

Before pulling myself up onto Morrow's outer deck, I put the ski mask on.

Up I went, triggering the motion-sensor light.

The crowbar got the sliding door open with a quick snap.

And an interior alarm started shrieking.

With a pen flashlight I made my way through the house.

A light clicked on in a room at the end of a hall.

I turned off my flashlight and stepped into a bathroom.

A beam of light hit the hallway.

He had a flashlight, too.

As soon as the light passed the bathroom I jumped and got who I figured was Morrow in a nasty headlock.

It took only a second to find the gun in his right hand.

I took it from him and said, "Turn off the alarm now or I kill you."

"Okay, okay! But they'll come!"

"Now," I said.

He went to a code pad by the front door. He turned on a light. Punched in a code. The alarm stopped.

"Please don't hurt me. Or beat me up."

"Call the company and tell them it's a false alarm," I said.

"Do you want money?"

I touched the gun barrel to his head. He yelped. He was wearing a silk bathrobe, open over boxers. I hope never to see that sight again.

"Call them or you—"

"Jonny?"

A sleepy woman's voice coming from the bedroom.

"Tell her it was a false alarm," I said.

"False alarm" Morrow said. "Be right there."

"Good, Jon," I said. "Now you call the alarm company."

The theme from *The Magnificent Seven* chimed.

"That's my phone," Morrow said.

"Answer it," I said. "And call them off. Or I shoot you both."

We went into the bedroom. I shone the light on the bed. A little blonde with big blue eyes squinted at me. She looked no older than nineteen. She had the black satin pulled up to cover herself.

Morrow answered his phone.

"No, I tripped it by accident," he said. "Sorry. My code is QQ8883 … yes … thank you."

"Turn on a light," I said.

He did. A painting of nude woman sitting in the lotus position and looking up at a rainbow hung above the bed.

"What's your story?" I said to girl.

"Don't shoot me," she said.

Jon-Scott Morrow gave her a disgusted look.

"Sit on the bed, Jon," I said.

He sat.

I took off my ski mask.

"Good God," Morrow said.

"Just your neighbor," I said.

The girl said, "What's this about?"

"Is he paying you?" I said.

She nodded.

"Do you have a car?"

She shook her head.

"Uber?"

She nodded.

"Give her the money," I said to Morrow.

Morrow curled his upper lip. Then he opened the drawer to the bedside table. He pulled out a roll of bills, took the rubber band off, peeled five bills and put them on the bed. They were hundreds.

"Is that it?" I said to the girl.

"Yeah."

"Give her a tip," I said.

"What?" Morrow said.

"Another hundred," I said, and tapped his skull with the gun.

Morrow plunked down another bill.

I handed the money to the girl.

"Thank you," she said. "Do you party?"

"Only if there's a clown making balloon animals," I said. "Get dressed."

I WALKED MORROW out to his living room so the girl could get dressed. I made him sit on the floor.

"Please don't let any of this get out, it'll kill me."

"I might do the same."

"Please," he said. "Can I call my agent?"

"You don't get to call anybody."

"I can't let anything happen to the movie."

I almost slapped him just for saying that.

I said, "Where is Brooklyn Christie?"

"I don't know any ... "

"You had a party here a couple of weeks ago, isn't that right?"

"I have parties sometimes."

"Wednesday, two weeks ago."

He thought about it. "I had some people over."

"Brooklyn Christie was at that party, Jon. Tall, long dark hair. A friend of Lindsay DeSalvo."

"I sort of remember."

I tweaked his skull with my index finger. "Try harder."

He rubbed his head. "Don't do that!"

I did it again.

"Ow!" he said. "Come on!"

"She tried to kill herself that night," I said. "Or somebody poisoned her."

"Dear God. Not here."

"How do you know?" I said.

"I just ... I would know."

"Were you drinking that night?"

"Sure."

"Drugs?"

"A little grass maybe."

The girl appeared in the foyer. "The car's on its way," she said. "I guess I should wait outside."

"Don't call the police!" Morrow said. "Whatever you do."

"You're not going to shoot him, are you?" the girl asked me.

"I didn't see his last movie," I said. "So maybe not."

AFTER SHE CLOSED the door I said, "When I found Brooklyn on the beach, coming from the general direction of your house, she said something odd. It sounded like *higog*. You know what I think she was saying? Hickok. As in Wild Bill. As in the movie you're slated to do. Also listed in the cast is Lindsay DeSalvo. Now, tell me again you don't know who Brooklyn is."

"Okay, yes. I remember her. I didn't talk to her, except to say hello. She was with some older guy."

"Who?"

"I don't know."

"Can you describe him?"

"Gray hair, a producer type. I think they had a fight. He left."

"Who did you spend your time with?"

"Lindsay, mostly. We had a thing going."

"A thing?"

"You know."

"You're a real romantic, Jon."

"I liked her! I really did."

"You gave her a part in your movie," I said. "Was that for services rendered?"

"Come on," Morrow said, almost squealing.

"How did you meet Lindsay?"

He didn't answer. I could tell he could have.

"Did Claude introduce you to her?"

"So what?"

"Do you know about Tanya?" I said.

"I don't know these people you're talking about."

218

"Tanya Camarasa," I said.

He shook his head.

"Don't lie, Jon."

"I'm not! I swear!"

"Did Lindsay ever talk about an angel named Michael?"

Jon-Scott Morrow issued a heavy sigh. He shook his head. "Why don't you just ask Lindsay about all this?"

"I think you know why."

His eyes widened. I saw fear there. Though whether it was out of guilt or confusion I couldn't tell.

"Lindsay DeSalvo is dead," I said.

"Dear God!"

"You've got that line down, Jon."

"How?"

"Claude."

"No way! He wouldn't."

"Where does Claude live?" I said.

"Huh?"

I tweaked his head again.

"Ow!" he said.

"Where does Claude live?"

Morrow said, "He rents a condo. About two miles from here."

"Get your car keys."

"What? Wait—"

"You're going to drive me there."

"I can't. He won't like it."

"Jon, let me assure you, he is not going to care."

I WALKED MORROW to the door connecting the garage. Inside was a beautiful red Ferrari, a car he did not deserve.

"You drive," I said.

On the way there he kept talking, in a high-pitched voice

219

that almost killed some of my brain cells, that he hadn't done anything wrong, that he was trying to get his life back together, that everything was tied up in this new movie, that—

"Enough," I said. "You buttered your bread, now jam it."

"What ... does that mean?"

"Live with the consequences of your actions, and quit whining about it."

He didn't say anything else until we got to a condo complex half a mile off PCH. All was quiet. Morrow pulled into the rear of the complex, pulled up near a back door.

"That's it," he said.

"Turn off the car." I said.

"What are you going to do?"

"Now."

He killed the engine.

"Get out," I said.

"Why?"

I held up my tweaking finger.

He put his hand up. "Okay!"

We approached the door together. I had the crowbar with me and got ready to use it.

"You can't do that," Morrow said. "He has guns."

"He's not here," I said.

"What?"

"Be quiet and do what I tell you."

I broke us in and turned on the lights.

THE PLACE WAS neat, which didn't surprise me. Sociopaths are often the neatest people on the block.

Living room spacious, with a TV the size of a truck on one wall. Everything was done in dark colors, down to the black carpet. A German Iron Cross medal, framed, hung on the wall opposite the TV.

"Why isn't he here?" Morrow said.

"Because he's dead."

The actor put his chubby hand over his mouth.

I pulled his arm down and guided him down the hall.

"But how?" he said.

I didn't answer.

"Did you?" he said.

Silence from me. I turned on the lights in the bedroom and looked around. There was a set of dumbbells next to the king-sized bed. A desk with a laptop on it, and a poster of skull breaking out of a swastika.

I grabbed Morrow by his bathrobe and shoved him down onto the bed.

"This is the last time I'm going to ask you nicely, Jon. Don't lie to me."

"Please, dear God, you've got to believe me."

"No, I don't."

"I don't know what Claude did on his off time. Please, can we get out of here? I really need to sleep."

I backed off and looked down at his pitiful form.

Then I grabbed the laptop.

"What are you doing?" Morrow said.

"Drive me back," I said.

In the Ferrari he said, "Please, this can't get out. I can't have my name connected with any of this."

"If I find out you're lying, Jon, that will be the least of your worries."

"What are you going to do?"

"To you?"

"Yes!"

"Like a good suspense movie, Jon, you'll have to wait and see."

I GOT BACK to my place at two a.m. Woke up at eight covered with sweat and filled with a Samuel Beckett-type emptiness.

Waiting for Godot.

Or the other shoe to drop.

I got in the shower and listened to my mind. It was a circus in there. I was one of the clowns, running around in a circle.

Where was Brooklyn?

Was she dead or alive?

The last two people to see her were both dead.

I should not ever be put in charge of witness protection.

What was up with the video? Why was it made? For laughs? For someone to see?

Why the body switch?

Cue circus music, and start it all over again.

No answers, only questions.

Just like Socrates.

Pass the hemlock, friends.

What did this Tanya the angel-gazer have to do with all this?

Was Jon-Scott Morrow as innocent as he said he was?

He still deserved to be punched several times in the face.

Is that your business, Romeo? Leave those faces alone.

Can you?

Make some coffee and figure out what to do next.

You're going to need Ira's help.

But Ira does not do violence like you do, Romeo. He gave all that up.

Maybe you should, too.

But you know you can't.

Sophie. What are you going to do about Sophie?

She's already decided for you, hasn't she?

Love lost. Maybe you should write a damn poem about it.

The Cavalier poets can eat my shorts.

I WAS DOWNING that first cup of joe when I heard a gentle knocking at my screen door.

It was Artra Murray.

I slid the door open.

"Morning, Mike."

"Artra. Coffee?"

"No thank you. I just wanted to check. How's the girl? Brooklyn."

"You better have that coffee."

She studied my face. "Okay."

We sat on the two chairs on my porch. The morning sun was just starting to warm the Cove.

I gave Artra the story.

When I finished she shook her head and said, "Evil."

"You don't hear that word much anymore," I said.

"It's a watchword for our times," she said. "I've seen it all my life. What are you going to do, Mike?"

"I'm thinking that through," I said.

"You're a thinker, I know that about you."

"Maybe it's a curse. I—"

I stopped when I spotted someone running along the beach. Running like someone trying to get in shape.

It was Carter "C Dog" Weeks.

"You were saying?" Artra said.

"Maybe I should believe in miracles," I said.

"I do," she said. "Keep believing."

AFTER SHE LEFT I started looking at Claude's PC. I knew I'd have to take another shower after this. The desktop wallpaper was a black and white photograph that history buffs would immediately recognize—the 1934 Nuremberg Rally, with the three huge Nazi banners in the background and the tens of thousands of people on the sides. And a tiny Adolf giving his salute in the foreground.

How sweet.

I tried a search for the word "Brooklyn." Three matches, but each one turned out to be a reference to the city.

"Lindsay DeSalvo" turned up nothing.

Then I tried "Donahue." One hit, a reference to Phil Donahue in an email sent to Claude back in April. Was Phil Donahue still alive? I shoved that irrelevant question out of my mind.

I took a quick look at his emails and knew it would be a Herculean challenge to go through them. I decided I'd ask Ira to help me figure out a systematic approach.

A little after eleven, Ray Christie called me.

"Haven't heard from you in a few days," he said.

I had to withhold the whole truth from him. At least for now.

"I've questioned several people," I said. "I plan to question several more."

"Why is it taking so long?"

"There are pieces missing," I said. "I'm trying to fill them in."

"Are you?" A sharp-edged tone.

"I am, Ray."

"How do I know that? How do I know how you're spending your time?"

"I've been keeping a log. I can—"

"So? How do I know you're telling the truth?"

"Let's meet in a couple of days," I said. "I'll give you a full report."

"She's dead, isn't she?" he said.

"We don't know that," I said.

"You're not telling me something. What is it?"

"There's nothing that confirms Brooklyn is dead, Mr. Christie."

"Confirms? Then she might be?"

"We both know that's possible. But we don't give up."

"I want to know what you are doing to find my daughter!"

When I didn't speak right away, Ray Christie said, "I'm sorry. I didn't mean to lose it. I mean, I did, but I can't … I haven't slept …"

"It's okay. Give me two more days and let's meet."

"Two days?"

"Yes," I said.

There was always that miracle.

ONCE, WHEN I was fourteen and a freshman at Yale, I was assigned to do a paper analyzing the thought of Plotinus as it related to the advance of medieval philosophy. Eager to impress, I spent a sleepless two days poring over the *Enneads* and, at the same time, jumping into major secondary sources like John N. Deck's *Nature, Contemplation and the One* and Ralph Adams Cram's introduction to the *Historia Calamitatum* of Peter Abélard. I got so much information crammed into my head during that forty-eight hours, I could not think straight or sideways. I fainted from exhaustion and was taken to the Yale-New Haven hospital.

When I came out of what seemed like a deep, dark, visionless sleep, there was a pattern in my head, a complete picture. It was as if I had been spreading around jigsaw puzzle pieces with oven-mitted hands for two days, then went to sleep, only to wake up and discover that the puzzle was completed.

I got a ninety-eight on the paper, and realized for the first time the power of the cells in the cellar, the subconscious mind, when given a hard job to do.

Which is why, at a little after noon, I went on my own run.

Just to clear the cobwebs and the muck, to let the cells do some work.

I didn't go the way of the Morrow house and the Malibu millionaires. I'd had enough of those fumes. I ran up the bluff to where the air was cleaner.

After about five miles I was back at my place. My plan was to lie on the floor and wait for the pictures.

I had not planned on a man in a suit with bow tie, waiting on my porch.

HE WAS SHORT, with wire-rim glasses and the smile of a movie studio accountant. The yellow bow tie and light-brown suit were out of place here at an L.A. beach in November. They would have been more fitting at a summer regatta in Nantucket.

He was sitting on my porch and stood when I got there.

"Mr. Romeo?" he said.

"That's me."

"My name is Markham." He extended his hand and I shook it. "I work for Mr. Zane Donahue."

"Oh really? I'd love to have a word with Mr. Donahue."

"And he with you. May I discuss the particulars with you?"

"Who are you?"

"I'm his personal assistant. Can we discuss this inside?"

"What's wrong with right here?"

"This is more in the nature of a business meeting, Mr. Romeo."

I shrugged. "If you don't mind a sweaty runner at your business meeting."

He smiled. "You'd be surprised at the appearance of some people at our meetings."

I unlocked the door and in we went.

Then I took a moment to slide the screen closed so the good morning sea air would waft in.

When I turned around, Markham was about ten feet away pointing a very large gun at me.

"Whoa," I said. "Is that a Magnum?"

"It is exactly," Markham said. "A .357."

"You fire that thing and a lot of people will come running."

"Get on your knees if you will, please."

"Come on, Markham."

"Please. Then I can make the call."

"What call?"

"To Mr. Donahue."

"Tell you what," I said. "I'll just make myself comfortable in a chair." I placed myself on the futon.

"We are reasonable people," Markham said, keeping the gun on me. With his other hand he took out a phone and thumbed it.

"All set," Markham said after a moment. Then put the phone away. "He'll be here in just a sec."

"Who?"

"Mr. Donahue, of course. Just remain calm."

"I'm calm as a napping Buddhist," I said.

"I was told to be concerned that you might want to try something. You are apparently a man of action. This show of force was only to make sure the situation didn't get needlessly out of hand."

"Can I offer you anything?" I said. "A Coke? Beer? Valium?"

"I'm good," Markham said. "And you will be soon."

That's when Zane Donahue came to the screen door and let himself in.

"Hello, Mike," he said.

My mind started churning up visions of taking both these guys out.

"What brings you to my humble abode?" I said.

"I think you know," he said. "Because if you don't, you're not as intelligent as I thought you were."

"Sure I know. You set me up. You're going to finish the job."

Zane Donahue shook his head. "I had to make sure you wouldn't fly off the old handle. Can I have your assurance you'll listen to me?"

"Sure."

"I mean really," Donahue said.

"I mean sure," I said.

"Good enough. Put the iron away."

Markham put his Magnum in what I presumed was a rear holster under his coat.

"Now," Zane Donahue said, "I have a feeling you may not trust me."

"Your feeling is correct."

"I came here to tell you I wasn't the one who gave you up," he said.

"And why should I believe that?"

"Because I'm talking to you, straight up, man to man."

"Used car salesmen talk the same way," I said.

"I used to sell used cars," Markham said, frowning.

"I was not the one who told them at Peniel you were coming," said Donahue. "It was Robin."

"So you say," I said.

"Yes, well, what can I say? Robin is no longer with us."

The way he spoke made it all sound credible. But I still wasn't buying the whole thing. Not yet. I would need more proof.

Then Zane Donahue gave it to me.

"BEFORE ROBIN LEFT my employ," Donahue said, "he gave me some information."

"Gave you?"

"Or rather was incentivized to provide it. How I do business is not the issue at hand. What is the issue is that I can give you the answer to your little problem. How you choose to use that information will be your affair."

"Why are you being so generous?" I said.

"It's a goodwill offer," he said. "I owe you something for what you went through because of Robin. The principal is responsible for the agent."

"Somehow I don't think goodwill is entirely what this is about."

"It's ninety percent of it," Donahue said. "You still have five hundred dollars of my money and, in a moment, an astounding piece of information."

"About that," I said. "There's been a little glitch with the five hundred."

"Glitch?"

"Stolen."

Donahue started laughing. "Oh man, you have had a rough time of it. Of course, that's not my fault, is it?"

"I guess not."

"You still owe me five hundred dollars of service."

"Maybe I'll just pay you back."

"No, you won't," Donahue said. "I won't take it. You're in my debt. I like it that way. And you will be further in my debt when you hear what I have to say. You will recognize the value of this information, and I'm counting on you to do the right thing to recompense me at some point in the future. Are we agreed?"

"I'll have to hear this information first," I said "Then I can decide if it's valuable or not."

"You will be blown away," Zane Donahue said.

"Not many things blow me away."

"Just listen."

I did.

And was blown away.

THE ANCIENT ROMANS, when they were strutting their stuff across the Western world, came to believe that chance events were really under the control of some form of deity. So they worshipped Fate, or Fortune, as a god. This god was fickle, and needed sacrifices to be appeased and prompted to bestow favor.

Machiavelli, on the other hand, didn't believe in Fate. There was no deity controlling the dice. We live in a world of chaos, and the only thing we can do is exercise our will over events.

Which is what I was about to do.

It was night and I was crouching in the brush at the top of Topanga, a spot with a breathtaking view of the west San Fernando Valley. The lights of that burg twinkled in their nighttime way. Christmas was coming. And so was a bomb.

Fifty feet below me, and slightly to the east, was a pad carved out of the hillside, upon which sat five heavy machines and the foundations of a new housing tract. I could see it all clearly. Ira's military-grade night-vision goggles, which he last wore in Syria nearly twenty years ago, did their work.

Zane Donahue had found out who the mad bomber was and when his next strike would come.

Tonight.

And also that Kalolo the bartender worked for him.

Doing what, I'd have to find out for myself.

The bomber's name was supposedly Jeffery and he was someone very few people knew that much about.

I was going to find out as much as I could.

If Donahue's intel was accurate.

And if it was, I would have a whole new respect for Zane

Donahue, the way one respects an alligator. He said there would be two of them, Jeffery and a confederate. I was not to harm the confederate, because he was the one who had supplied the information to Donahue.

I was not to inquire as to how Donahue got the confederate to turn, but I assumed money had changed hands. And maybe a threat.

I was dressed ninja style, in black sweats. The top was a windbreaker. A good thing, as the chill winds from the ocean blew by me and down into the valley.

It was right about two in the morning, just when Zane Donahue said it would happen, that the two men scurried onto the pad. The one who was not Jeffery was as Donahue described. Short and stocky. He held the flashlight.

Jeffery looked athletic. The way he ran, the way he was carrying something like a football. The device, I presumed. To blow up the heavy machinery and send another of his messages.

I started making my way down the hill.

THIRTY SECONDS LATER I was on the pad myself, hidden in shadow.

The two men were in the middle of a foundational pour, with the construction equipment surrounding it. Jeffery squatted over something, while the other stood and watched. Like they were about to start a campfire.

Or set a bomb.

I pounced.

With one hand I pushed the squatting bomber to his back and gave him a kick in the ribs, administering enough pain to incapacitate him for a moment.

Then I turned to the confederate, who looked scared, even

though he knew I wasn't going to hurt him. I made a fake lunge at him and he dropped the flashlight and ran off.

Leaving me with the groaning Jeffery.

I took off my goggles and picked up the flashlight. Then I knelt and pulled Jeffery to a sitting position. Put him in my favorite hammerlock, a variation I'd learned from my first teacher. By crooking his arm and placing the side of my hand on his elbow, I had complete control over him with just the slightest pressure of my left hand. I could dole out the pain as I saw fit.

With my free hand I shined the flashlight in his face. He closed his eyes at the light. I got this odd sense that I knew this guy, but the equal sense that I didn't.

"Hello, Jeffery."

"Who the—"

"We're going to talk," I said. "But you're going to disarm your device first."

He winced into the light. "Who are you?"

"The archangel Michael. I command you to defuse the bomb."

Jeffery had a momentary face freeze. He didn't like being hosed. These types never do. The good ones recover in a few seconds. Jeffery was a good one. "Not going to," he said.

"Then we'll go up together," I said.

"Yeah, we will."

Keeping the hammerlock on him, I shifted to a sitting position.

"I'm not joking, man," Jeffery said. "I'm ready to die."

"For the great cause?" I said.

"Maybe."

"You're going spread your guts on this hill because of carbon emissions?"

"You don't know anything," he said.

"Well, at least blood and intestines are biodegradable."

He blinked a couple of times.

I said, "You don't really believe that archangel Michael jive, do you?"

Silence.

"Ready to die?" I said.

He tried to look defiant.

I said, "Death is the undiscovered country from whose bourn no traveler returns."

He looked away from the light.

"Hamlet," I said. "He asks, who would grunt and sweat under a weary life if it weren't for fear of what happens after death? You said you're ready to die, so you must not be worried about it."

"Yeah, I said it."

"I'm good with that. I'm the same way. What are the options? We could simply lose consciousness. Cease to exist. Or we could come back in some kind of karmic way. If that's true, I'm pretty sure you're going to be a cockroach. You've killed people."

"Some people deserve to die," he said.

"And you get to make that call? Let's see how that works out in the afterlife. There could be a hell. Pretty strong tradition for that. Eternal punishment. I'm pretty sure, according to that plan, you're going to be turning on a spit."

"Shut up."

I pressurized his arm. He howled.

"I'm kind of interested to see what happens," I said. "Maybe I can communicate through a Ouija board to some high school freshman."

"You're really going to die, man."

"I'm counting on it."

"This thing is going to go off," he said.

"Let's talk about the existence of the cosmos itself. Do you think it came from nothing? Or—"

"I'm telling you! It is going to go!"

"Like the big bang," I said. "Do you think there was a cause for the big bang?"

"You're crazy!"

"Let's talk about that," I said. "There are those who believe crazy is only a term placed upon what is behaviorally inevitable. What's your view of determinists?"

I could feel his body starting to shake.

"You know," I said. "I've changed my mind. I don't want to die yet."

"Yeah, see?"

"So I'll render you unconscious and leave you with your little device. I'll go and do some research on biological necessity and the nature of existence."

He opened his mouth.

"Good night, Jeffery." I wrapped my right arm around his neck and began to squeeze.

HE TAPPED OUT a few seconds later.

I let go the pressure and let him cough in some air.

"You wanted to say something?" I said.

"Okay," he said. "Just don't kill me."

"I don't want to kill you, Jeffery. Far from it."

"Then what's all this?"

"Defuse the device," I said.

I let him go so he could crawl over to his bomb. I shined the flashlight on it to make things easier. The only sure way to deactivate an explosive device is to have the guy who made it do it. You don't get many chances like that in life. I did, and it worked.

"Okay," he said.

"Take it apart," I said.

"It's off."

"Jeffery, take it apart or we go back to limiting your air."

When he cursed, I knew he hadn't disarmed the thing. So I watched patiently as he broke it down into its components.

"Satisfied?" Jeffery said.

"Oh no," I said. "Sit facing me."

He did. I put the flashlight on him again.

"Let me see your wallet," I said.

"What?"

"Wallet. ID check."

"I don't have my wallet. You think I—"

"Then I pat search you. If I find that you do have your wallet, I break your arm."

He gave me his wallet.

I checked the license. The name on it was Timothy Railsback.

"I thought your name was Jeffery," I said.

"You called me that."

"Why would you be using a fake name, Jeffery?"

He said nothing.

"I don't like liars," I said. "Do you want to know what I do with liars?"

"No," he said.

"Tell me about Kalolo."

"Who?"

"Kalolo Tuputala."

"I don't know anybody named that. What do you want from me?"

"The truth, Jeffery."

"I'm not Jeffery!"

"Let's go home and find out," I said.

That's when Jeffery made his last desperate move.

HE KICKED OUT at me, falling backward as he did.

He got the flashlight and it was solid enough to dislodge it from my hand. It was a lucky kick, but I should have been ready for it. He looked in pretty good shape.

And proved it by scampering fast off the foundation.

I grabbed the light and turned it back in time to see Jeffery's behind duck around a big cat.

I picked up the night-vision goggles and put them on and took off after him.

By the sound of his steps I was able to get a direction, followed, then saw him as he jumped off the pad and into the darkness.

KIERKEGAARD WROTE ABOUT a leap from uncertainty to certainty, from unbelief to faith. Mine was the opposite. From solid ground to hillside, from footing to flight. But Kierkegaard only had oil lamps. What might he have seen with night specs?

I jumped over the side of the hill and landed with a skid. The scrub brush was heavy. I paused for a scan. It was not hard to pick him up. He was about twenty yards down from me, moving like a scared rabbit.

Looks like I was hunting again after all.

He went down, too.

I jumped and landed just above him. He was on his side, looking up at me.

I felt no remorse.

And put Jeffery to sleep.

GETTING HIM BACK up the hillside was another hassle. It's one thing to carry an inert body over level ground, or in an octagon before you slam him to the canvas. It's another to drag a worthless punk up a steep incline. But the legs did their duty. I reached the pad, walked across it, then went up another incline to where my car was.

It was actually a pretty good workout.

I opened the trunk. There were some lengths of nylon rope in there. I hog-tied Jeffery and with an oily rag I gagged him. Checked his pockets and pulled out a set of keys. Then I put him in the trunk and closed it.

Good old classic Mustang. No emergency release inside the trunk.

I went back down to the foundation and gathered the explosive device parts and the wallet. Back at Spinoza, I tossed my goggles in the back seat and put the bomb parts there, too. Got in behind the wheel and took another look at the license.

The address was in Agoura, California. I decided to find out if it was real.

THE HOUSE WAS at the end of a street in a high-end development.

I drove across the lawn and practically up to the front door.

Grabbed a pair of gloves, got out and unlocked the front door.

Stepped in and felt for a light switch.

I was in a nice-sized, home builder's idea of a foyer.

No security keypad that I could see.

Which I thought was curious. For about four seconds.

Then I discovered a good reason why he didn't need one.

The click-clacking of paws on tile got louder as a pit bull scampered into the hall.

We made eye contact.

And then the dog did what it had been trained to do.

NOW, I LOVE dogs. Except shelties. Shelties are the snooty neighbor of dog breeds, perpetually ticked off that they are not collies, with a loud, brain-scraping bark that goes off with the slightest provocation. Unless you are the loving owner, a sheltie will not give you the time of day unless you give it a Liv-a-Snap, and maybe not even then.

I'll take a pit bull over a sheltie.

Or a German shepherd.

Unless it's a German shepherd that has been trained to chew your face off.

Like this one.

Up to this moment I had never faced a dog in mortal combat. But I'd run a scenario through my mind on several occasions.

You're not going to do much good standing still. You have to move at just the right moment, and hope you can grab a leg.

Oh yes, and keep your arm out of the jaws of death.

It would help to have pepper spray or a weapon, but I hadn't brought either along. And there was nothing to grab.

All this flashed through my head in as the dog ran at me with its chompers.

I juked it. Like a running back I gave a quick move left just as the pitter prepared to leap.

It went for my fake and pushed right.

All of its legs were off the ground for half a second.

I made a grab for one of the hinds.

It slipped through my hand.

The dog hit the floor and skidded to the front door and didn't waste any time getting up for another charge.

I ran into the living room, faintly lit by the light of the foyer, looking for a sofa pillow or small table or anything I could grab.

Turned out to be a floor lamp.

And just in time.

The incisors from hell jumped from the small step right at my chest.

Holding the lamp like Little John's quarterstaff, I pushed it into the jaws.

Which clamped on the tube so hard, the thing snapped in two.

But the dog wanted flesh.

I wanted my flesh to stay exactly where it was.

We were not communicating.

Jaws fell to the floor, and I dropped with him. It was instinct on my part. I thought of the dog as a very small cage opponent with a big mouth.

Looking back, it was a stupid thing to do. I was putting my neck down to his biting space.

But I managed a headlock and rolled so the dog's feet were in the air.

The slow choking of his airways took the fight out of him.

I grabbed him by the back legs and walked, with him dangling, out of the living room.

In the hall was a closet. I opened the door and placed him on the floor and shut him in. I heard a whimper. That got to me. He was only doing what he'd been trained to do. He fought like a true champion.

I wished I could have told him that in dog language.

I FOUND MY way to an office. A desktop computer sat on the desk. Everything was neat and tidy. This looked like the house of a well-adjusted businessman, not a crazy, angel-believing bomber. If that's what he truly believed. Who knew?

I looked on the desk for random papers. There weren't any. I opened up the drawers and went through them. Nothing of interest. Office supplies, blank paper and envelopes, stickies, a drawer dedicated to candy, Lemonheads and M&Ms being prominent.

In the bottom drawer on the right, I found a small, glass enclosure. Like a little fish tank. Or greenhouse.

And I suddenly remembered where I had seen Jeffery before.

In a photo.

On the desk of UCLA professor Gary Pasfield.

His son, the All-American.

BRENTWOOD IS A fashionable district on the west side. This is where the successful sleep. At least according to the world's standards. At four in the morning, in the darkest part of the night, you wonder just how many alcoholics and wife beaters are snoozing behind impressive façades.

Because things aren't always what they appear to be, as I was about to find out and confirm.

I parked Spinoza half a block away from the house. Jeffery was still in the trunk. I opened it and told him to sit tight and not flop around and use up his air. It was a snarky thing to say, but I enjoyed saying it. I closed the trunk again.

I walked up to the house. It was impressive. Tuscan style. Neatly groomed yard illuminated by little lights strategically placed. A black Mercedes was parked in the circular driveway.

I rang the doorbell. Listened. Knocked loudly. Listened some more. Through the dappled glass on the upper part of the door a light flashed on. The sound of steps. The sound stopped and I knew someone was on the other side.

"It's about your son," I said through the door.

"Who are you?"

"We've met," I said. "Your son Jeffery is in trouble. We need to talk."

"I don't know what this is all about. I need to call the police here."

"You don't want to do that, Dr. Pasfield. Because the whole bombing thing is going to come out. Your son is going to talk. I think you better open the door."

IT TOOK ANOTHER couple of cajoles, but Pasfield opened the door. When he saw my face he tightened.

"You," he said.

"Me," I said.

I stepped in and closed the door behind me. Pasfield was dressed in a bathrobe and slippers. He looked like any grandfather on Christmas morning. But he had been naughty.

"What's this about my son?"

"Why does he use the name Timothy Railsback?" I said.

Rarely do you see someone's face actually go white, like they do in ghost stories. But I saw it happen right there in the entryway of Dr. Gary Pasfield's house.

Not only did the color drain away, but he looked like he couldn't move. He shook a little. Rumbling around in his head was the question of what to do. There was no answer.

Finally he said, "What do you want from me?"

"I will make this very simple," I said. "You are going to tell me where Brooklyn Christie is. If you don't, harm is going to come to your son."

Pasfield shook his head as if he couldn't believe what I was saying.

I took out my phone and called up the picture I had recently taken. It showed Jeffery, gag on his mouth, looking at me wide-eyed.

I held the picture up to him.

Any color that was left in Pasfield's face left for the Bahamas.

In a whisper, he said, "What do you want with her?"

"Then she's alive."

"What could you possibly want with her?"

"I was hired to find her," I said.

"I can pay you more, much more, to leave this alone."

"Not interested."

"You don't understand. I'm talking about real money. Big money."

"Where is she, Doc?"

He raised his chin. "We can work something out."

Disgust burned my throat. "I'm this close to working out on your face, Dr. Pasfield."

"I can give her to you," Pasfield said.

"Give her to me now."

"I'm not talking about Brooklyn," he said. His eyes were wide and spittle spray came out with the word. "I'm talking about Tanya. She's the one you want! She's the one who's running all this. I have nothing to do with it. I can give her to you."

"Brooklyn," I said.

"I don't know where she is," Pasfield said.

"Then you'll never see Jeffery again."

His breathing got harder. He looked like a fifth grader trying to think up a lie to his teacher. I just stood there and waited.

He closed his eyes. "You've got to give me some assurances."

"The only assurance I'm going to give you is that you get your son when I get Brooklyn."

"But she'll say things. You'll say things. You can't."

"Do you want your son or don't you?"

He actually appeared to be thinking this over.

Then, with a sigh, he said, "All right. But I want to know where he is right now."

"We get Brooklyn first."

"Will you let me get dressed?"

"No, Doc. I'm going to stay with you every step of the way. And if you make any move that I don't like, I'm going to be very upset."

"You have no idea the damage you're doing."

"Now."

He turned and started walking.

I followed.

MOST SOUTHERN CALIFORNIA homes don't have basements. But some of the higher-end homes do. Because of building restrictions, homeowners who reach a limit on the ground above can only add on by digging down. Basements, extra bedrooms, wine cellars.

Pasfield had one of these. I kept right on his heels as he went to a door off the laundry room. The door had a keypad lock. Pasfield entered the code and the door clicked open.

I took hold of the back of his robe. "We go in easy," I said.

We did.

Pasfield flicked on light. We went down a set of stairs.

At the bottom he turned on another light. We were in a bedroom. It was carpeted, windowless, and cold.

There was a king bed in the corner. It had an ornate headboard and bedposts, something out of Charles Dickens.

It also had Brooklyn Christie on top of it.

Her eyes were closed. She had no clothes. Her right wrist was handcuffed to a bedpost.

Dr. Gary Pasfield shot forward. I was left holding his robe. I went after him.

Pasfield jumped at the wall. His right hand grabbed some sort of fixture. He pulled it.

There was a crackling noise, then an explosion.
And the walls lit up with fire.

NO THOUGHTS, JUST action.

I reached Pasfield who had turned to face me. He smiled
at me like a skull. With one vicious right I took off the smile
and sent him to floor.

I turned to the bed where flames were starting to lick the
blanket.

Brooklyn's arm was cuffed to the narrow part of the lathed
bedpost. I grabbed the post with both hands and pulled.

It moved a little.

I put my foot on the bed frame and pulled again.

The post ripped free.

I scooped up Brooklyn, post and all.

As I made for the stairs I looked back at Pasfield. He was
on the floor. He was no longer dressed in pajamas. He was
wearing fire.

And screaming.

I GOT BROOKLYN outside and put her on the grass. She
was breathing slowly. She looked drugged. I ran back inside to
see about Pasfield. But the basement was blocked by a solid
wall of flame.

Outside again. Like the first time I saw her on the beach,
I put Brooklyn Christie over my shoulder. Only this time with
a dangling bedpost.

Which must have looked just a tad funny to the old man
in khakis and an undershirt coming up the driveway.

"What is this?" he said.

"Call 911," I said. "There's a man inside."

"Who are you?"

"Hurry."

I got Brooklyn to Spinoza, put her in the back seat.

Then drove out of Brentwood. Out of the darkness.

By the time I reached the Cove, the sun was about to come up.

I PARKED IN front of Artra's. Knocked on the door.

It took her a minute, but she appeared, belting her robe.

"Now what's happened?" she said.

"Brooklyn. She needs you. I don't want her in the hospital."

"Why not?"

"I want her safe. Keep her with you until I give the okay. Will you do that for me, Artra?"

"Only for you. Where is she?"

"I'll bring her in."

I used my lock-pick kit to get the handcuffs off Brooklyn. She moaned as I put her on Artra's sofa.

But she opened her eyes.

Then her mouth, as if to scream.

I touched her lips with my finger.

"It's okay now," I said. "You're safe."

I TOLD ARTRA what I could. Then drove to Ira's and knocked on his door.

Ira opened the door and said, "You're out and about early, my friend."

"I may need a lawyer," I said.

"Before morning coffee? Come in and—"

"Yes, before morning coffee."

"What is this about, Michael?"

"I have somebody tied up in the trunk of my car," I said.

Ira nodded. "Yes, you need a lawyer."

AS WE WAITED for the police to arrive, Ira had a go at Claude's computer. He was able, in just a few minutes, to unlock files that had pictures and videos of men and women in, let us say, compromising positions. The videos and pictures looked as if they'd been from hidden cameras.

Prominent in the pictures were Dr. Gary Pasfield, Jeffery, Jon-Scott Morrow, and others. A nice cache of blackmail waiting for the right moment. But for Claude, that moment would never come.

And he had set something else up, too. Ira and I were discussing it when the police arrived. I went outside, popped Spinoza's trunk, and handed over a screaming and unhinged Jeffery Pasfield.

The cops mentioned the word *kidnapping*.

Ira mentioned the California statute that permits a citizen's arrest in the case of a felony. He then showed them some of the evidence on the laptop.

One of the uniformed officers told us to "sit tight."

Half-an-hour later, the detective team of Vic Baker and Soledad Molina arrived. I had not treated them with much deference the last time they were here. Their expressions told me they remembered it well.

Ira suggested we all sit down with some tea.

Baker and Molina agreed only to sit down.

Ira said, "We've been piecing together a rather complex web of activity. But if you've ever wanted one of those sensational cases that make careers, this would be the one."

The detectives tried to look objective, even skeptical. But Ira's soothing, authoritative voice had made a dent.

"There is a big picture and smaller pictures around it," Ira said. "The evidence we'll hand over to you will corroborate it all. I suggest you take all this down."

"You mind if we record it?" Detective Molina asked.

"I would appreciate it," Ira said.

Molina removed a small, digital recorder from her coat pocket. She pressed a button and put it on the coffee table.

"Okay," she said.

Ira said, "We begin with the mountain community called Peniel. All cults need a magnetic personality at the center, and Tanya Camarasa fits the bill."

"How do you spell that?" Detective Molina said.

"I'll print it out for you anon," Ira said.

"A what?" Baker said.

"Soon," Ira said. "She gathered her minions, as cult leaders have done here in Southern California for over a century."

"I can agree with that," Baker said.

"They were ostensibly about loving the earth, expressing that love through Dionysian enthusiasms."

"Excuse me?" Baker said.

"Referring to the pagan god Dionysus," Ira said. "A pursuit of non-rational ecstasy."

"Beating drums and dancing around," I said.

"Ah," Baker said.

"With chemical and cannabis enhancements," I said.

"And further," Ira said, "there is some high-end sex trafficking. You'll have plenty to work with here. Tanya has a client list and Claude was apparently the go-between. Claude also worked security for Jon-Scott Morrow. But I believe it was because Tanya had something on Morrow, wanted leverage over him for something."

"What might that be?" Baker said.

"I suspect Morrow would be useful to her among the Hollywood set. More clients, you see."

I said, "And Morrow had been resistant. Which is where Brooklyn Christie comes in."

"The missing woman you told us about," Molina said.

"What I'm not sure about is her connection with Desiree Parks," I said. "And why Ms. Parks was beaten."

"She's recovering," Molina said. "We've only been able to talk to her once. She said the man who beat her up was named"—she consulted a small notebook in her left hand—"Kalolo?"

"That would be correct," I said.

"And you know this how?" Molina said.

"I'll get to that," I said.

"We haven't been able to find him," Baker said. "If you know anything ..."

"A strange tale will unfold," I said.

Baker and Molina frowned in tandem. They were like two synchronized swimmers.

"Before that," I said, "something about Brooklyn Christie. You're going to want to question Jon-Scott Morrow."

"The actor?" Molina said.

"He's going to be a little nervous," I said, "because he has a big movie coming up. But don't let that stop you."

Baker said, "We never have before."

"From what I've seen," I said, "my theory is this guy Claude poisoned Brooklyn at Morrow's house, in the morning hours after a party there. The idea was to make it look like a suicide. This would make Mr. Morrow look very bad indeed. You'll have to grill Morrow on what he knows, but he'll fold like a lawn chair. Maybe he found her and got her to vomit, on purpose or accidentally. Maybe somehow she vomited on her own. Whatever, she ended up on the beach where I found her. Probably Morrow set her loose out there in the fog, so she wouldn't be found in the house."

"We should talk to Brooklyn Christie," Molina said.

"When she feels up to it," I said.

"Where is she now?" Molina said.

"Being taken care of," I said.

"Why are you being vague?" Baker said.

"It's his way," Ira said. "But she is a client of ours, so I would ask your indulgence for a day. We will contact you tomorrow."

"Why tomorrow?" Baker said.

"Because," I said, "we have an appointment to keep today."

TWO HOURS LATER we were inside Ray Christie's room at the exquisite Motel 6 on Sepulveda. The décor was mid-century orange. Ray Christie's face was middle-aged ashen.

I gave him the news that Brooklyn was in a doctor's care.

"Thank God," he said. "Please take me to her."

"Better sit down first," I said.

"What? Why? What's happened?"

Ira, using his crutches, went to the chair by the window and sat.

"What is this?" Ray said. "I want to see Brooklyn."

"Not just yet," I said. "Sit down."

He looked at Ira, back at me. "I don't understand."

I said, "A little matter to clear up concerning your relationship with Dr. Gary Pasfield."

"Who?"

"You'd better sit down, Mr. Christie," Ira said.

Ray Christie paused, then lowered himself onto the bed.

"You told me you didn't know Pasfield," I said. "But you and he were high school classmates in Indiana."

Ray said, "I don't know what you're talking about. I want to see—"

"I was doing some background on Pasfield," Ira said. "I

like to find visuals whenever I can. Did you know your high school yearbook is online, photos and all?"

Ray Christie's Adam's apple bobbed.

"You didn't have a very large class," Ira said. "Imagine my surprise to find your name there."

With a chest starting to heave, Ray Christie looked back at forth at Ira and me.

Ira said, "So I looked through Pasfield's laptop. He wasn't very good at encrypting emails. Is there another Ray-CDrywall at AOL?"

Ray Christie said nothing. There was nothing he could say.

"Five years ago your business was in trouble," I said. "There was even an item about that in the Arizona Republic. One of your employees sued you for workplace harassment. His name was Fisher. Morton Fisher. He accused you of anti-Semitism."

"That was never proved!" Ray Christie said.

"You settled," I said.

"Because it didn't happen," Ray said.

"After the bad publicity, you needed money. And you got it. From your old classmate Gary Pasfield."

Ray Christie was starting to breathe hard.

I said, "You asked Pasfield for a loan, and he asked you for Brooklyn. To be his assistant in some environmental work. How'm I doing so far?"

He stared at the floor.

"It wasn't long before Pasfield introduced Brooklyn to Tanya," I said. "And they went to work on her. Drugs were part of it. They broke her down, filled her head with that neo-pagan gibberish about angels. And got her involved in a sex racket. A business partnership between Tanya and Pasfield, with Jon-Scott Morrow as one of their best customers. We'll get more when Brooklyn can talk to us."

Ray Christie started to weep.

"When did you find out what they'd done to her?" I said.

Barely above a whisper, Ray Christie said, "A year ago."

"Did you use a private detective to find out?"

He nodded.

"And Pasfield found out, told you to back off. Threatened you. And Brooklyn."

Another nod.

"So Brooklyn called you and begged you to help her. She mentioned my name. You decided I was the right guy to try to find her and take the heat, even if it meant death."

"I didn't ..." Ray sobbed "... mean for it ..."

"Brooklyn wanted to get away from Pasfield. Pasfield made her his own personal—"

"Please don't," Ray Christie said.

"He even went so far as to fake her murder. He must have paid Claude and the big bartender a nice sum to do that."

Ira looked at me from across the room, gesturing at me to go easy.

"Then there were the explosions," I said. "You knew who was behind them. Pasfield and his son. They really thought they were saving the earth, too."

Ray Christie was silent.

"You knew because Brooklyn told you," I said. "She found out that Pasfield was involved, but not Tanya. Brooklyn trusted her. That's why she went back to her after she was poisoned."

"I don't know anything about this," Ray Christie said.

"You do," I said, "because of that crazy screed that was published, implicating the Tanya angel cult. Remember we talked about that?"

Ray's eyes were like a guy in front of a firing squad.

"You wrote that yourself. You wanted the cops to have a long look at Tanya and Pasfield. But you couldn't help slipping in something about the Jewish state. Your little marker."

Ray Christie shook his head slowly, several times. Then he put his head in his hands and said, "What am I gonna do?"

Ira got out of his chair, crossed the room on his crutches. He sat on the bed next to Ray Christie.

"Let me tell you something about my religion," Ira said. "Something that may get you to cut us a break. Can I tell you?"

Head still in hands, Ray Christie nodded.

"We teach three things that lead to forgiveness. The first is repentance, the acknowledgement of one's wrong. I think you're there. Next, one must go to the person wronged and *ask* to be forgiven. The third thing is to undo as much of the damage as one can. Do those three things and you'll find healing walking right alongside you."

For a long moment, no one said anything.

Ira said, "Maybe we Hebrews have learned a few things over the last five thousand years."

Ray Christie looked up from his hands.

TWO DAYS LATER the story of the Tanya Camarasa sex ring operation broke wide. Based in large part on Ira's evidence from the laptop, and a breakdown by Jeffery Pasfield that resulted in what the law calls a spontaneous inculpatory state-ment, the whole scheme was to raise money for the operation of Peniel and contributions by the inmates there to the cam-paign of Allison Ursula Serret.

The *Los Angeles Times* refused to mention that last part. Instead they referred to "unsubstantiated rumors" potentially planted by "political enemies" of the "development crowd."

Jon-Scott Morrow's name got mentioned. I wondered, this being Hollywood and America today, whether the news of his sex romps might actually revive his career. When I finished reading the story, I took a shower.

Brooklyn Christie talked to the police. I was with her when

she did. She wanted me there, and as Ira's investigator I could claim attorney-client status. She corroborated some of the key evidence. She broke down a couple of times when she spoke about the drugs and the life she'd been roped into.

I HELD HER hand.

When we were through, I walked her outside where Ray Christie was waiting. Brooklyn's hand tensed in mine. She looked at me, as if to ask if it was all right to let go. I nodded.

She kissed me on the cheek.

And then, without a word, she turned to her father.

He had tears in his eyes.

Brooklyn put her arm around his shoulder. Ray Christie wept into her chest.

I took my leave.

THE NEXT MORNING I was sitting on the beach at Paradise Cove, waiting for the sun to come up and break through the dark clouds, looking out at the ocean and not feeling much of anything. The events of the past couple of weeks had carved an ice sculpture out of my chest. I couldn't quite make out what the sculpture was supposed to be.

I wondered if it looked like Jason Pratt, the guy who was trying to out me in L.A.

Or maybe it was me, frozen in time.

Then I remembered it was Thursday. Sophie would be at the bookstore later that day.

But if it was her, that sculpture was melting away.

"What's up?" Carter "C Dog" Weeks landed with a plop in the sand next to me.

My fists were balled and one was raised. "Don't ever do that to me, C. I almost dented your face."

"Easy, dude. I only came out to tell you I'm clean a week."

"Truly?"

"I got all this energy all of a sudden."

"Like a puppy dog," I said. "Maybe that should be your new name."

"No, please!"

"A week you say?"

"I went to two meetings," he said.

"Then I've got a present for you."

"My guitar?"

"The very same."

He threw his arms around my neck and dove into a hug.

"Thank you, man!" he said.

I gave him a man pat then peeled him off.

C Dog let out a whoop, picked up a handful of sand and threw it toward the water.

"Now I'll do you a favor," he said.

"What's that?" I said.

"You looked sort of down, out here all alone. Like you got troubles. Why don't you tell your buddy C Dog about it?"

"That's real nice, C, but—"

"Woman trouble?" he said.

"Now why would you think that?" I said.

"Because I'm the love doctor," he said.

I started laughing. It was too much. A wiry sometime musician, former pothead—at least for the moment—wanting to counsel me on the ways of romance. It was so fresh and naive I just couldn't let him down. So I told him all about it, about Sophie, about giving a beating to her boyfriend, about how that was what probably turned her off. Heck, it helped a little just to say it.

"Then you got to go back to her, man," C Dog said. "And win her over."

"Yeah?"

"She sounds worth it. You're not the kind of guy who gives up without a fight, are you?"

I laughed again.

I said, "Did you know I can catch a Frisbee with my teeth?"

"Like a dog?"

"Better than a dog."

"Cool!" he said.

"Want to play some?" I said.

"I'll go get my disc," C Dog said, standing and shaking sand off him.

"Awesome sauce," I said.

He smiled big and ran off.

I laced my hands behind my head and lay back on the sand, looking at the dismal cloud cover over the beach. There was a little bit of a silver glow to it. The sun was back there somewhere, pumping fire.

About the Author

James Scott Bell is an award-winning thriller writer, and the #1 bestselling author on the craft of fiction. He is a graduate of the USC Law School and U.C. Santa Barbara, where he studied writing with Raymond Carver. He is third-generation Los Angeles, where most of his books are set. Visit his website www.jamesscottbell.com

CPSIA information can be obtained
at www.ICGtesting.com
Printed in the USA
LVOW03s0242160617
538228LV00003B/21/P